Driftfeather on the Alaska Seas

Ultimate Future of the
Past--Another Alaskan Mystery

Marianne Schlegelmilch

PO Box 221974 Anchorage, Alaska 99522-1974
books@publicationconsultants.com—www.publicationconsultants.com

ISBN 978-1-59433-318-7
EBook ISBN 978-1-59433-319-4

Library of Congress Catalog Card Number: 2012942361

Cover Art by Barb Montpas Sirmeyer

—First Edition—

Manufactured in the United States of America

In memory of Shadow Schlegelmilch,
the Best Dog on Earth

Chapter One
Beginning from the End

The divorce had been acrimonious—unexpectedly, to say the least, and not helped one tiny bit by the fact that Mara's now ex-husband had brought Sassy's daughter, Erin, to the proceedings.

Perhaps it had been some kind of skewed karma or something, since it had been she who Doug had left Sassy for, although by no means had she been instrumental in that happening. Now he had left her.

No, it had all been out of her control, she having just arrived in Alaska from the South-48 when they met—flung, along with Doug and all those close to him, into the melodrama of international proportions that had marked her first two years in the place many called the Last Frontier.

Erin certainly hadn't looked pregnant anymore when she had seen her at the proceedings this morning. Not that that was a tragedy. Being free of any memory of her cruel rape at the hands of the drug lord who killed her mother was probably a good thing for someone as young as she, no matter how well-intentioned she had been about accepting the circumstances of her life. Why, and under what circumstances, nearly 40-year-old Doug Williams had become entangled with the daughter of his ex-lover was the real mystery.

She shrugged as the scenario played out in her head. Why should she care? She and Doug were now officially divorced, and he had chosen to not even show a final increment of respect by bringing his young paramour to the courtroom.

She had personally handed their wolf-dog, Thor, over to him on the way out of the courthouse, and it had been hard. She and Thor had always had a close bond and having him with her as she readied her house for sale and packed for the move to Juneau had been her only joy since Doug had shocked her with the news that he was leaving her.

Doug wanted Thor back, and since Thor was originally his dog she didn't resist. She and Thor would always be connected—and that was a fact. She had told Doug more than once, and in no uncertain terms, that if he ever changed his mind about keeping Thor, he should find a way to get him to her—no matter what it took to find her. She would try to believe that he had listened.

According to the court clerk, it would take two weeks before the paperwork making the change to her maiden name would be final. Somehow that made it all the easier to drive down to the glacier-fed Knik River south of Palmer and let the SUV Doug had bought her for her last birthday roll into the river. By the time any of them knew about the "accident," she would have filed a report on the lost vehicle, claiming that she had, in her distraught state, accidentally forgotten to put it in park when she had stopped near the river to mourn the end of her marriage.

The newspaper would later report the accident and that she was okay, but by then she would be well on her way to Juneau with none of those who had been her Alaska family aware of how or when she would get there. Although, for some, the act could be viewed as immature and overly dramatic, Brad Edwards had left her a wealthy widow and the sacrificing of the SUV accomplished the dual purpose of freeing her from another memory of the man whose pledge to love her forever had been as empty as he had left her heart, and of securing her freedom from those who she knew might try to find her.

At least Doug had been decent enough to forfeit any claim to her assets—a relief in view of his otherwise contentious behavior as of late. The new truck and camper she purchased before leaving Palmer the next day would serve to take her to a new life, free from all the horrors of the past two years.

As far as her friends in Palmer, those with whose lives she had become tightly entwined, having hidden Doug's activities with Erin from her—well, they would have to be part of the past. Whether intentionally or not, they had betrayed her.

Never again would she trust as much as she had this time. Except for Thor, none of them mattered anymore—or so Mara Benson's head tried to silence her heart.

Chapter Two
Chance Encounter?

"Boy, I didn't see that one coming either, Jane," a woman at the next gas pump from where Mara was filling up in Glenallen said.

"Sal?"

"Well, I ain't Elizabeth Taylor," Sal answered, laughing. "Although Joe says I coulda been back in the day."

"Is Joe okay?" Mara asked.

"More 'n okay," Sal answered. "I'll tell 'im ya asked. Better yet, you tell 'im."

Just then, Joe Michael walked up to his new model one-ton dualie pick-up and wiped a speck off the front chrome bumper before turning to acknowledge her.

"You' re gettin' to be kinda high maintenance, young lady," he laughed.

The sound of Joe's Native Alaskan accent erased any qualms she might have had about taking this brief detour from her travels. The old man, who had mysteriously walked into her life almost two years ago, soothed her just by his presence—the gentleness of his voice a steadying reassurance that there was some kind of sanity and rationality in life.

Joe looked grayer now. Maybe it was because he had exchanged his black-rimmed eyeglasses for a more modern rimless pair. She mentioned the change, complimenting him on his new appearance rather than focusing on the added gray hair.

"Kinda miss my old ones," he said, pushing on the bridge to move the glasses up his nose. "But Sal says these are sexier."

Joe's lighthearted wink said it all.

"Don't ya be an old fool now, sweet baby," Sal said with mock sternness.

Mara smiled at seeing the love the two shared. The woman who had taken her in so many times when she was in need, and who affectionately always referred to her as "Jane," had ended up being the love of Joe Michael's life.

If someone who had been through what Joe Michael had in life could find love again, then maybe there was hope for people like her. After all, at least she hadn't lost her entire family to a fire, nor had she fought two combat tours in Vietnam like Joe had. Then again, hadn't the stress she had faced in losing Brad in a plane crash, finding him alive under an assumed name in Alaska, and then seeing him murdered before her eyes been just about as traumatic as what Joe had been through? And now there was the divorce . . .

"Well, gotta get down to the VFW for taco night," Joe said, climbing onto the running boards of his truck and sliding onto the seat.

She watched Sal nudge Joe on the arm and lean over to whisper something in his ear.

"Oh . . . yeah," she heard him say.

"If ya got nothin' goin', why don't ya join us?" he said out the rolled-down truck window.

"I don't know . . ." Mara hesitated.

"C'mon, Jane," Sal said. "Ain't nothin' ta be embarrassed about with the divorce."

How did Sal know about her divorce?

"Look, Jane," Sal said. "Some guys just think they know what they want and some think they don't, and some just drift around tryin' to figure out which way they think. But it all comes down to the fact that some guys just can't handle knowin' they found a good woman, and so they revert back to what they think they want, and more often 'n not, that means hangin' with some skank. Now, don't get me wrong, I ain't sayin that's what happened with yer man—especially bein' as he hooked up with a babe with bucks, but, on the other hand, skank is as skank does and so—I'm just sayin' . . . "

She laughed at Sal's description of Doug and Erin. Certainly Erin De la Corte was a girl—a woman—of breeding, but, historically, she had shown a tendency to display poor judgment in her choice of men. Hadn't her birth mother, Sassy, been just the same way?

Maybe character formation was genetic? Why else would a woman like Erin just not know any better even in the face of outstanding upbringing? Sassy was another story, but Erin? Well, that question would be better left to others. She was certainly no psychologist.

As for Doug, well, what could she say about him? He had been through hell in the past couple of years. First the murder of his brother, then his failed relationship with Erin's mother, Amanda Carlson, the loss of his beloved seiner—and along with it, his chosen lifestyle.

Doug Williams had proven himself to be a man lost. Why she, as his wife and closest confidante, had not been able to pull him through the tragedies that weighed so heavily on him—a fact made all the more hurtful by his choosing of a questionable relationship with a woman young enough to be his daughter—was the real mystery, or was failure a better word? But, then, wasn't that just like her—to always take the blame for others' misfortune? As if reading her mind, Sal leaned over Joe, and called out the truck window.

"Ya can stand there mullin' it all over till ya implode, Jane, but the bottom line is that we all got choices, and yer guy, Doug, made his. When ya stop blamin' yerself for everyone else's thinkin', then maybe ya can move on with findin' yer own happiness."

Mara looked at Sal. The woman was scary in her ability to see into her mind.

"We'll see ya over ta the VFW," Sal said. "Jest turn left at the corner and then left again about a half mile up. You'll see it. There's about twenty flags along the front. Can't miss it."

She waved to the two as they drove off. Maybe she would just continue down the road. When she saw the flag-lined one-story rectangular building with Joe's truck sitting out front, she slowed, sped up, then suddenly whipped left into the parking lot, where she pulled up beside the light gray dualie, got out, and went inside.

Chapter Three
The War

Joe Michael was leaning on one elbow against the long wooden bar inside the VFW when Mara walked through the door. Holding her breath in a futile attempt to escape the fumes in the smoke-filled room, she walked up and stood beside him.

Joe was talking with the bartender, a sixty-something man with the moderate paunch and gray-bearded face so typical of his generation of Vietnam veterans. Seated alone, at the far end of the bar, a sinewy oldster sat wearing a ball cap that listed the unit he had fought with in World War II.

"Buy my man, Joe, here a drink," the oldster called out, struggling to catch his breath before taking a long drag on his cigarette.

"Ya know I cut way back on drinkin' while you still could stand up without yer walker, Murph," Joe called to him playfully.

"Yeah, so ya said. Damn Nam vets—rather suck in somma that illegal funny stuff than take a good respectable drink," Murph called back, signaling the bartender to give him a refill on his whiskey.

"Thanks all the same now, Murph," Joe laughed. "You just make sure ta call yer daughter to come get ya when yer ready to go home, okay?"

"Yeah, sure, but she ain't gonna like it none," Murph muttered.

"You ready to go home, Grandpa?" a young woman called from the doorway to the bar.

"Now who in the blazes told ya ta come git me, granddaughter? As in if I didn't already know that yer mother's hell-bent on bein' the same killjoy as'n her own mother—God rest her sainted soul—was."

Stubbing out his cigarette, Murph gave an exasperated half wave to no one in particular and joined his granddaughter at the door.

"C'mon, Grandpa. You know Mom's got dinner waitin' for ya at home."

"I was gettin' ready to think about headin' back jest afore ya got here. Weren't no need fer yer mother ta send . . ."

Murph sputtered and spewed as the door clunked closed behind him. Mara laughed at seeing the way the old man became docile in spite of his gruff demeanor. Seeing all the men who had congregated in this place with those like-minded, many with hats or caps identifying their status as war veterans, made her think of her own father.

He had died when she was nine, making him virtually a stranger to her except for the memory of how he had always brought her something bearing the likeness of an eagle every Christmas—each time telling her the bird was the proud symbol of his Army unit, and prompting her to think of her father every time she saw one of the magnificent birds that were so plentiful in Alaska.

"Tell me about my father," she said, sliding onto the bar stool next to Joe.

"Bring us a coupla beers, would ya?" Joe Michael said to the bartender, before turning to face her, all the while looking down as he talked.

"Your father was a hero, Mara. Most everyone who was there was a hero. It's just that in this case, he was my hero. Like Sal told ya—he kept me from steppin' on that land mine.

"It was near Thanksgiving in '66. Our platoon had just finished a mission outside of Tuy Hoa and were making our way back to base camp when your father, who was walkin' point, signaled us to stay back. I was walkin' right behind him and for some reason I had been lookin' down and missed the signal.

"I called to him in a whisper, just like I always did, and told him I was comin' up on his right. Just as I was about to step forward, he threw himself sideways, knockin' me off the trail, which was at the top of a small rise. I tumbled down the far side of it, landin' at the bottom just in time to avoid the blast . . ."

Joe's voice had become low and his speech hesitant. Although she couldn't be sure in the dark, smoky haze of the bar, she thought she saw a tear fall onto Joe's cheek and looked uncomfortably away.

"Your father came rollin' down the rise right behind me and nearly landed right on top of me," Joe continued, wiping his eyes before laughing wryly.

"At first we grabbed onto each other to try to steel ourselves against the concussion from the blast. For a minute I thought I was deaf. It wasn't long before I knew I wasn't.

"You never heard cussin' the likes of what yer father unloaded on me right there—tellin' me to never follow the point man that close again, and lucky I didn't get the both of us killed by doin' somethin' that stupid—and a few other choice words you're better off not hearin'."

For several minutes, neither of them said anything as Joe took a couple of swigs of beer, and she sat trying to picture the scene he had just described.

"Too bad he had to die the slow death by poison that Agent Orange gave him," Joe said, somberly.

She placed one hand on Joe's arm as she watched him fight back more tears and struggled to hold back her own.

"I just gotta believe that they didn't know it would kill us all," he said, looking her straight in the eye. "Our own government. We were fightin' for them and for everyone in our country and everyone held under oppression in Nam. To think they were using somethin' that could harm us as we served—takin' that kind of chance—well, I just can't let myself think they would take that kind of risk. I could never live with believin' that and I want you to believe that, too, Mara—that they never knew they were killin' good men like your father and all the rest when they sprayed that defoliant in the jungles we were fightin' in."

"I never knew him or my mother," she said simply, taking the focus away from Joe's obvious ambivalence about the truth. "He just never talked much, especially after Mom died."

"That's why ya got me," Joe answered, "and now ya got Sal, too. Your father—he was more a brother to me than my own no-g—"

"Looks like them tacos is ready fer us," Sal called from a nearby table, stopping Joe from finishing what he had been about to say.

Swallowing the rest of his beer, Joe slid off his bar stool and Mara did the same.

"So what ya got goin' in Juneau?" he asked her, his usual lightheartedness returning.

"Well, I've got a job offer and I'm going to buy a house and—well—try to start over again," she answered.

Picking up her plate and extending it for the food server to fill, she suddenly turned to Joe and said, "That's just a line of bull, Joe. The truth is, I do have a job offer, but I have no idea how I'm going to feel about it when I get there."

Joe chuckled. "That's what I like about you, Mara. You got the heart of the brave."

She looked at him before breaking out in a smile of her own.

"Thanks for noticing," she said, winking.

For the next two hours, she sat with Sal and Joe, first eating homemade tacos and then helping to move the tables and chairs so the dancing could begin. By the time Joe had finished whirling her around the floor of the VFW until she felt dizzy, it was close to 9 p.m.

"Are ya sure ya gotta go, Jane?" Sal said.

"If I don't, Sal, you're never gonna get a chance to dance with your husband."

"Well, unless I stop him, he'll be here till two days from tomorrow," Sal laughed.

"I was hoping to see Della on the way out of town—and her mother," Mara said.

"Since the shooting, Della pulls all the curtains the minute the light leaves," Sal answered. "Probably not a good idea to turn up and surprise her."

"Is she doing okay?"

"Joe thinks so, but woman to woman, I think it changed her—made her less trusting, more of a stay-at-home, ya know?"

Mara bent down and held a paper napkin open with one hand while she carefully wrote on it with a pen she pulled out of her pocket.

Hi Della,

I'm just passing through, and I wanted to visit, but Joe and Sal kept me here at the VFW long past a decent hour to come and see you. I hope you're doing okay and I hope you still have the feather I left for you—the one that Joe gave me that saved my life. I'll try to see you if ever I'm in Glenallen again. And please tell your mother that Thor still has the medallion she made for him on his collar and I still wear my matching quill bracelet every day.

Love,

Mara Benson (used to be Williams—just got divorced—long story)

Carefully folding the napkin, she handed it to Sal, asking her to please give it to Della the next time she saw her. If she had turned around, she might have seen the young Native woman with one arm in a sling watching her from the kitchen.

Chapter Four
Clean Break . . . Almost

Glenallen had been pleasantly weird. Seeing Joe and Sal again had brought a sense of calm to Mara's quest to escape the chaos of the last two years—chaos that had further tangled emotions she had come to Alaska to unravel in the first place.

Too bad she had missed any opportunity to visit Della. It would have been nice to see her. Hopefully, Della would at least know from the note written on the napkin that she hadn't forgotten her—as if that were even possible. You don't forget something like what they had been through.

When she got to Tok, she checked into a new motel along the highway at the Tok cutoff located at the junction of the Alaska and Glenn Highways. The town was a small but significant crossroads to all comings or goings between Alaska and Canada, and this motel hadn't been there the last time she had been through.

That time, she had been staying across town at another motel when the same thug who had raped Erin had shot Della in the parking lot during his murderous attempt to flee Alaska. Thankfully, she wouldn't have to stay there again. After all that had happened, if there could have been any way to avoid Tok at all, she would have taken it, so the newer motel was her best option under the circumstances.

After unpacking her clothes, she took out her cell phone and saw that the message box was full. Pulling up the *delete* prompt, she stopped herself from pushing it, hesitated for several seconds, and then pressed the *play messages* prompt instead.

When she got to Juneau she planned to get a new phone and new number anyway, so she might as well let her personal drama finish playing out on this one—right? Besides, as much as she told herself she didn't care, she wanted to know who, if any, of her old friends was calling.

Unsurprisingly, the first call was from Sarah and the second from Ellie. After listening for a minute, she pushed *fast forward,* not wanting to hear the rest of their frantic explanations about how they had known about Erin, but had been powerless to intervene.

When she lifted her finger to let the playback resume, she was stunned to hear Doug's voice:

Mara, the divorce hit me harder than I thought it would. Bringing Erin there was stupid. When I heard about the accident after you left the courthouse . . .

A sudden beep cut off Doug's message. Mercifully, her voice mail was full. Who was Doug trying to kid anyway?

Stabbing fitfully at the keypad, she finally managed to press *delete*, and then she pressed it again for good measure to make sure the messages were gone.

Restless tossing and turning for half the night robbed her of much needed sleep. Would she ever shake loose from the past? She and Doug were divorced and the fact that he had taken up with Erin was what it was and completely out of her control. She should have just taken Thor. Why did any of this matter anymore anyway? But why shouldn't it? Anyone would feel the same. Finally, giving up on sleep, she took a long hot shower and checked out of the motel.

A thin white coating of frost covered her windshield, foretelling the coming of winter. Although the sun had not yet risen, she could see a brilliant thin orange line along the horizon that told her it wouldn't be long before it did.

Shivering inside her SUV, she waited for it to warm up. While she sat there, she opened the long sealed envelope that Sal had given her as she left the VFW. Sal had told her to wait until she got to Tok to open it, saying it was from Joe. Unbelievably, it contained another feather almost identical to the one he had given her on the ferry over two years ago when they first met, only this time, instead of one red dot being painted on the upper third of the outer edge, there were two. Was it an eagle feather? She wasn't sure. Joe had scratched his name onto the quill in tiny black letters and listed its origin as "Tok, Alaska."

On a scrap of brown paper tucked inside the envelope was a brief handwritten message:

The worst is closer than you think.
As your own strength grows,
mine will begin to fade.
As before, keep this to protect your future,
but this time the danger will be from my past.
Joe Michael

The note was somber, and it lacked Joe's rhythmic tone of the past, which alarmed her. She tucked it into her bag and tried not to think of it, all the while knowing that Joe's words should never be ignored.

Then, impulsively and purely out of some sense of duty to their long friendship, she called Sarah back, heaving a sigh of relief when a recording said she couldn't come to the phone right now, and to please leave a message.

"Sarah, this is Mara," she began, measuring her words carefully. "I got your messages. I got everyone's messages . . ."

She held back from saying too much, from telling the woman who had long been her best friend about the betrayal, and about how hurt she had been to learn what they all knew. Unlike she had done in the letter she had sent Sarah from Bellingham when she had first left for Alaska, she avoided mentioning that she was off to a new life. This time she would not explain.

After a long pause, she simply said, "Give B.D. a hug for me," and hung up.

She would have to live with not knowing the baby that Sarah had named for both Brad and Doug. In the biggest way, naming the baby represented the depth of the friendship she and Sarah had shared, but it was time to let it go. Somehow deep down she knew that.

Forcing tears back, she shoved all thoughts of Sarah, the baby, and both of her former husbands into some recess of her mind. A few miles down the road, she stopped at the nearest store and bought a disposable cell phone, slowing to toss the old one into a dumpster on her way out of town.

No one heard it ring from its resting place in the bottom of the empty giant green receptacle, nor could they hear Sarah's muffled reply to her message: *Mara! I was just changing B.D.'s diaper. I couldn't get to the phone. Call me back. Please. You'll always be my best friend. I'll wait right here . . .*

Then she drove out of town leaving the last physical remnant of her past behind. For the rest of the trip she would be Jane Brown, just in case one of them decided to put out a missing-person bulletin on her or something.

In Juneau, she would officially begin her new life. This time, though, that new life would be hers and hers alone.

Chapter Five
Juneau Office

On first impression, the Juneau office of Ocean Research and Preserve in Juneau lacked any of the charm that had first endeared Mara to its Homer counterpart.

"What was it you said your name was?" an austere-looking woman asked as she peered over horn-rimmed half-glasses that were balanced partway down her nose. "It'd be nice if they told us about transfers before people show up."

"It's Jane—Jane Brown. Please don't let this take away from your busy day. I'll contact the home office again and see if I can straighten this all out."

Slowly, she slid out the door as the woman, still muttering, sifted through a stack of papers behind her. Things weren't much better at the hotel where she had made reservations.

"Sorry, Miss, but we're filled up for the special session of the legislature. Seems like a lot of folks are pretty interested in having their say this session," the desk clerk said unapologetically.

"But my reservation was confirmed . . ." Mara said, pulling a folded piece of paper out of her purse.

"See here where it says confirmation only valid until 2 p.m. on the scheduled day of arrival?"

The clerk pointed impatiently to the fine print at the bottom of the confirmation letter, fussed with some papers for an inordinately long time, then put his pen down with painful slowness, before directing her attention to the clock on the wall behind her.

"It is now 3:15 p.m."

Well, wasn't he just a specialist in customer nonservice! Why even bother to try to reason with him? Better to spend her time looking for a room. When she failed to find one, she drove to the outskirts of town and parked her camper along a riverbed; tucking back into the brush as far as was possible so as not to be easily seen. In the morning she had an appointment with a realtor. Hopefully, she would find something soon.

Thankfully, she had filled the camper's supply tank with propane before getting on the ferry. She used the built-in microwave to heat one of the several frozen bowls of soup she kept in the freezer for times such as this. When she was done, she used half her tank of fresh water to take a long, hot shower before going to bed.

During the night, a pack of wolves howling off in the distance kept her from restful sleep, their sound seeming to be closer and closer as the night wore on. Once she thought she heard something brush along the camper near morning. Maybe the sound had been a bush moving in the wind or something, but it had frightened her and kept her on edge. When she stepped outside at first light, large, fresh doglike prints in the frost confirmed that the wolves had been all around her.

When a full day's search for a house turned up no likely prospects, she returned to the camper and did the same as she had done the night before. The next morning, she found a dump station and emptied her waste tanks. Finding fresh water was a little harder, but she managed to locate a place and filled up the camper holding tanks, before returning to the secluded spot that had become her temporary home.

When the realtor showed her a two-bedroom bungalow near the waterfront a few days later, it was not exactly what she was looking for, but she took it anyway, paying cash and closing the deal the same afternoon. In a strange twist, it kind of reminded her of Sal's place, but it wasn't Sal's place, it was her own, and for right now it more than suited her needs.

She slept in it the first night, awakened when she heard the wind howl down the woodstove pipe. Sleeping on the floor in the unheated cabin had shown her that even a sleeping bag good to 10 below was not the comfort she was used to, leaving no doubt that her first priority would be to buy some wood.

It was a definite plus that the bungalow was second to the last in the long row of homes-on-pilings that reached out to the edge of the harbor—sandwiched in unobtrusively, yet still close to the end, where it should be quieter than near the street.

She had slept soundly on that first night in spite of the cold, hearing nothing but the gentle lap of the waves under the cabin and the patter of bird feet on the roof once morning arrived. She even saw an eagle sitting on one of the posts that supported the docks, making her thoughts shift momentarily to the comforting conversation she had had with Joe about her father. If she could not enjoy knowing her own father, then Joe Michael was just about as close to a father as she could imagine.

The boardwalk that held the cabins was wide and extended about six feet beyond the face of the cabins to allow people to access their homes, and even to roll carts or drag sleds carrying their things to their doors.

A long ramp that rose and fell with the tides led from that boardwalk down to the first grid of docks in the harbor, but access was restricted to homeowners—at least according to the sign posted on the side of the first cabin.

She could see the harbor out both the front and back windows, and at high tide, as she had already learned, the water came right underneath her cabin, sometimes bringing with it an otter or two floating lazily in the kelp. Out her back window was a view of the backside of an identical row of cabins that sat about thirty feet away on another set of pilings, and held separate access to the harbor.

There was also a place out on the street to park her truck—her own designated spot with a sign that said, *reserved for #5 - B Row* next to it. Although it was out of view of her cabin, at least she had the security of knowing it was her own space—and the area was well lit with, according to her realtor, regular security patrols at night.

The cabin, as did each of them that lined this dock, had a room-sized porch out the back door that was surrounded with decking that stood about four feet high with room at the bottom to allow for water drainage and snow removal. The deck itself was uncovered.

It had already proven to be a perfect place to have coffee in the mornings. Perhaps something like latticework around the outside might be nice for privacy? No, that would feel too closed in. Tomorrow she would go shopping for a small table and chairs for the porch—one with a large umbrella to keep off the nearly constant rain that Southeast Alaska was known for. Maybe even, in the spring, she would consider having someone extend the roof over the porch—or not—or maybe she would just leave things as they were. For now, this was home, and there would be plenty of time to make it just right.

By week's end, just like any of a number of locals she had seen sitting out in the foggy mist, Mara sipped her morning Kona, comfortable in her felt-lined knee-high rubber boots as she propped her feet up on the wooden bench that the previous owner had left on the deck. Nestling inside her favorite wool sweater, she leaned back against the cedar wall of her cabin, obscure, anonymous, and one with the harbor scene.

When she went back inside and shook the drizzle out of her hair, it once again fell into the soft curls that she no longer tried to control—her weather-generated new look, but one that suited her well.

The drapes that lined the patio door provided all the privacy she needed for those times when she was in the mood for seclusion. Not that that was a bad thing. Being alone had already become an unanticipated guilty pleasure. The deck had plenty of large pots around the edge that she would fill with plants in the summer so she wouldn't have to use the heavy drapes as often, and could better enjoy the long summer days.

The cabin had come with a boat slip, too, although it was only large enough to hold a dinghy. She had already added *dinghy* to her mental wish list, so this time she mentally underlined it, too.

According to her realtor, an old man, a retired fisherman with a reputation for being as crusty as the bread he liked to make for his neighbors, lived in the cabin next to hers—in the last cabin in her row. She had already seen him coming up the ramp from the docks a few times, or standing alongside the railing smoking a pipe—or sometimes a stogie.

Impulsively, a few days after moving in, she knocked on his door and introduced herself as his new neighbor, Jane Brown.

"Well, around here, I'm known as Stu, uh, er, uh—Jane," he said, emphasizing the name and winking knowingly. "You did say you call yerself Jane, didn't ya?"

She contained any reaction to Stu's codgerly skepticism, nodded a yes and extended her hand to shake Stu's—a move that apparently deemed her worthy of an invitation for some hot tea and a piece of Stu's homemade bread.

"Jest pull up a chair, Jane," Stu insisted, pointing to a small, round table next to the window that overlooked the harbor. "Best bread you'll eat around here and might as well share some tea and take the chill outta yer bones."

She could see that from this vantage point, Stu had a bird's eye view of all who came and went at this end of the harbor.

"It's quiet here, 'cept when it ain't," Stu said matter–of-factly, sitting down in his chair at the table and tearing off a hunk of the steaming bread before passing the plate to her. "But mostly it's quiet here and so I stay."

She furrowed her brow a bit before smiling, nodding, and thanking Stu for the hospitality.

"Yep. It's more'n quiet here most times. Well, that is if ya don't consider runnin' off the occasional sea lion a bother—though to be truthful with ya, I ain't seen many in the harbor the last year or two."

"I was rather hoping for a quiet life," she said, trying to assure him that she would be an acceptable neighbor and was of a like mind about solitude.

She certainly was in no mood for any more drama in her life. Stu was an old sourdough and if he said he was managing all right, chances were good she would be able to as well.

While Stu got up to heat more water for the tea, she started thinking again about her plan to buy a gun and take shooting lessons. It was as good a time as any to get started with that, especially in view of all the chaos that had come her way since moving to Alaska—and even before. Now that she was alone, it was more than ever a matter of security.

What she wouldn't do—couldn't do—any longer was to depend on someone else to take care of her.

"It's good to know you'll be around if I need some help," she told the old man as she thanked him for the visit and made her way to the door, "but I think I should be all right."

Chapter Six
Past Present—Again!

On the advice of her new gun safety instructor, Mara picked out a 9mm semi-automatic pistol at the local gun shop. The information she provided would link all her names to anyone who had access to the information, but it was a privacy risk she would have to take. Fortunately her permit was approved without delay.

She would continue to go by Jane Brown around town and address any confusion about who she was on a case-by-case basis. Eventually her identity as Mara Benson would become known—especially once she found a job, but she would try to live discreetly until everyone from her past had moved on with their lives and had given up looking for her.

Right now a job was the furthest thing from her mind. At this point, after the reception she had received at the local OR&P office, as much as she had loved working at the Homer location, she had all but decided that this branch would not be her preferred place of employment.

When she saw the red and blue flashing lights in her rear view mirror, she looked around to see who had broken the law. Realizing that she was the one being pulled over, she slowed her vehicle and eased it over to the shoulder of the road.

"License and registration, please, ma'am," a uniformed police officer said matter-of-factly.

"What did I do?" she asked as she reached into her console for the documents.

"I got you going 51 in a 45, ma'am."

"But— " she began, before he interrupted her.

"I'll check these out and be right back," he said.

She watched the officer in her side mirror as he walked back to the white SUV with the large law enforcement emblem on the doors. A few moments later he returned, handing her back her license and insurance papers along with a citation for speeding.

"I could give you a warning, Ms. Benson, but I've decided that I'm going to give you a speeding ticket because I've been too easy on speeders recently and decided to crack down today."

"But I have a perfect record and—" she began, but the officer, whose nametag read K. Lessis, just shrugged and proceeded to tuck his clipboard under his arm.

"Sorry, miss, just doing my job."

Officer Lessis's forced smile failed to conceal his authority as she took the ticket from him.

"One more thing, Ms. Benson. I saw in your profile that there was a missing person's report lifted from you a couple of days ago."

A missing person's report? Was Ken Tandry trying to find her? Darn Sarah, anyway. Hadn't the phone message she left for her made it clear that she did not want to be found?

"And I see you filed for a concealed weapons permit, too," Officer Lessis continued.

What was going on? How would he have access to that information already? Wasn't that a federal matter?

She sat uncomfortably while Officer Lessis stared at her for what seemed like a full minute before reaching into his shirt pocket and handing her his card.

"If you need any assistance, Ms. Benson, please don't hesitate to contact me."

"I'm fine, officer. Thank you for your concern."

Why was he standing there staring at her again? Didn't he believe her? How had he learned about the gun permit and why had he mentioned it? It was probably something to do with some new law or something. Who could keep up with these things? From what she had seen, gun ownership rules seemed to always be changing, depending on the political whims of the day.

Finally, to her immense relief, Officer Lessis nodded and walked away.

"You drive safe now, ma'am."

"Damn," she muttered under her breath once he was out of earshot. "Juneau isn't turning out to be much in the way of a trouble-free new start."

Chapter Seven
Inside Scoop

"I see ole Lessis got ya," Stu said as he stood against his railing watching a seal swim around the harbor.

"How'd you know about that?" Mara asked.

"Saw ya pulled over on my way to the doctor," Stu answered.

She looked at him and smiled wryly.

"Don't worry about it too much—ya know, let it ruin yer day. Now that Lessis got ya once, he'll leave ya alone. Word is he's leavin' the force anyway. Heard he's goin' to work for some group from Outside. Heard it had somethin' to do with workin' for his wife's brother."

"Really," She forced herself to respond. All she wanted to do was forget about the ticket and Lessis and the uneasy feeling he had left her with.

"That's right, Jane. It's a true story—at least so the story goes," Stu answered, his deadpan expression accompanied by a wink.

"Well, it is what it is, Stu, so I guess I was in the wrong place at the wrong time, wasn't I?"

Good grief! Now she was starting to talk in clichés, too.

She laughed out loud at the thought, causing Stu to chuckle as well. There was just something comfortably familiar about Stu. Even in spite of his tendency to try to put his own suspicious spin on just about everything he took note of, she liked him. They should get along just fine—as long as she could learn to take whatever he said with a grain of salt.

She had always done that—taken people at face value and trusted their inherent goodness. Stu was an old man and he had come from a generation with a different value system than today's—one in which people carried a wryer sense of humor than did those in these more ominous modern times. She wouldn't worry about him and would choose to enjoy knowing him with all his quirks instead. Lessis, though, seemed like a different breed and so she would heed her inner voice and give him a wide berth.

Tomorrow she would pay the fine on the ticket and get on with her life. She had better things to do than worry about a minor traffic citation, although she would definitely be using her cruise control regularly from now on, leaving Officer Lessis and his counterparts time to fight more serious crime, and leaving her free to pursue her fresh start—hopefully without any more bumps in the road.

Chapter Eight
Home Sweet Home

The next day, after paying the fine on her ticket, Mara went to the DMV and got her driver's license changed to her new name and address. When she got home, she contacted her insurance company and updated them on her information. While she was at it, she changed the vanity plates she had been using back to the standard Alaska plates of gold with dark blue lettering, and then, since there was no room to park it, took her camper to a local campground that offered storage.

It would be easy enough to go pick it up if she decided to take a trip, but for now, there would be plenty to do exploring the waters around her new cabin in the new inflatable boat that she was supposed to pick up as soon as she bought a hitch for her pickup to haul it home on its trailer.

"You're gonna want a 12-footer with a fixed transom and a soft bottom if you think you might be using it out on the open ocean," the salesman had told her, "and this 25-horse outboard should serve you well."

On his advice, she selected the boat he had recommended, which fortunately was on sale that week for 10 percent off its regular price, and came with an upgraded trailer, repair kit, and pump.

She also purchased four Coast Guard-approved life preservers, although she more than likely would carry only one—maybe two—due to the size of the boat, unless she planned on having other passengers.

"I'll have our boatman splice a poly bowline to the boat for you and teach you how to tie it. We like to use polypropylene because it doesn't absorb water and it floats. It'll be more dependable that way."

She nodded in agreement, trying to look as though she thought the information was important. Well, it wasn't that it wasn't important, but shouldn't all those tiny details be best left to those whose business it was to outfit her properly?

"Uh-huh," she nodded as he talked. "Yes, I see."

"You'll see that the bowline's pretty short, and the reason for that is so that it can't reach the motor if it falls into the water," the salesman said. "I'll also have our man put an eye in the loose end. That way, if you ever need a longer line, you can connect it with a locking carabiner that you can pick up at any marine supply or hardware. I usually keep some around here just for that purpose, but we're sold out right now."

Later, on the advice of the boatman, she also picked up a 5-gallon bucket for bailing, and a cement-filled 3-gallon bucket that had an eye hook sticking out of the center of the cement, and to which was attached 4 feet of heavy chain and then 100 feet of nylon rope. She had seen Doug and some of the other fishermen use this setup for anchoring, and so she chose them from the stock in the store instead of investing in a fancier anchor.

Mostly she planned on tying the boat up under her cabin where she could access it through the trap door and climb down the ladder steps built onto one of the pilings under her cabin. Other than that, she would probably just beach it when she got to where she was going and float it out with the tide when she wanted to leave, so it was doubtful she would need an anchor all that often anyway. Still, you never knew, so she would carry one just in case.

"I sure appreciate all you've done to outfit me," she told the salesman.

"Well, when you're dealin' with the ocean, it don't make much sense to take shortcuts on your equipment," he said. "Besides, you seem like a pretty determined and adventurous woman, and we're happy to help ya out."

"Thanks again," she told him before walking out the door.

When she looked back, the salesman had stepped out the open back door of the shop and was filling a birdfeeder that she had watched a squirrel empty while he was explaining about the bowline. Thinking she might enjoy one, too, she picked up a bird feeder of her own on the way home, along with a bag of sunflower seeds to fill it with.

By week's end, all the modifications had been made and she accepted the store's offer to have her boat delivered and launched for the cost of their nominal delivery fee, saving her the hassle of trying to find someone to help her do it on her own.

The evening that it was delivered, she took a test run around the harbor with a technician, who showed her the finer points of operating the skiff before letting her bring it back in on her own while he stood by as back up.

Over the next week, she made several trips to stores around town, glad that she had her pickup to haul home the grill, patio table, and four chairs she found on sale at a local home improvement store.

One of her neighbors, a young fisherman named Alex, helped her unload them and haul them through the cabin and onto the deck out back. He even helped her hook up the propane tank to the grill and seemed more than happy when she offered him a sandwich and a beer for his efforts.

While she went inside to get the food ready, Alex checked out the setup for the inflatable, calling up to her, “Everything looks fine down here.”

Everything, it seemed, was finally moving along nicely in her new life in Juneau.

Chapter Nine
New Focus

"Yeah, I've had my eye on that seiner across the harbor there for about two years now," Alex told Mara later, as they lunched.

Pointing to a fishing boat he described as the third one from the end, he said, "About six more months and I'll be able to pay cash for her."

Mara looked in the direction Alex was pointing to. Sure enough, tied up along the third dock from the end was a light-blue seiner with a *for sale* sign in the window. Written in large green letters on both sides of the bow was the seiner's name, *Driftfeather.*

She listened as Alex described the particulars of the 48-foot seiner, including the fact that it came with a rebuilt Cat 365 horsepower diesel engine with only six hours on it, and a full complement of new or recently refurbished hydraulics and gear, three holds, and a recently remodeled cabin.

All of a sudden, her budding new life's path took an unexpected turn.

"How much are they asking for her?" She blurted out, her tone suddenly serious and businesslike.

"$325,000," Alex answered, "but I think I could get them down to $287,500—especially for cash. That's what I'd offer 'em—two eighty-seven five—not a low ball, but enough for the convenience of a cash deal."

"And how much do you have saved?" she asked, prompting him to lean intently forward at the insistent way she had asked the question.

"Close to $190,000."

Mara placed both elbows on the table, and looked Alex squarely in the eye.

"Although I don't have a lot of experience, I'm no stranger to purse seiners, Alex. And although I never met you until you were kind enough to help me haul my table and grill from my truck to this deck, for some reason I can't explain, I feel as though I've known you a long time."

Alex blushed and sat back in his chair. Hadn't he told her he was only twenty-four? She had already told him she was close to forty. He shot her a look of embarrassment as if to ask her what was going on here and if she was trying to hit on him or something?

"Look—geez, I don't even know your name, but—look, I'm not into . . ."

"Look, Alex, I wouldn't blame you for thinking that what I am about to say is both forward and strange . . ."

"Like I said—" Alex spat out, "I'm not . . ."

"Alex, I'm not talking about anything strange here. What I'm trying to say is, how would you feel about having a little help with buying that seiner?"

"But . . ." He stammered.

"Look, I'm talking about this being strictly a business deal," she said.

Alex shifted uncomfortably in his chair.

"I've got some money saved and I've been looking for a good investment," she told him. "Not only that, but I'm at a point in my life when I would like to go out to sea once in a while to work on some of my research projects—I'm a biologist—and maybe even go out fishing once in a while."

Alex leaned forward, focusing on her words. Maybe this was the opportunity he had been looking for. The timing certainly couldn't be any better. This was no time to act like a postpubescent manboy. He straightened himself in his chair and offered her his best businesslike demeanor.

"What I'm not interested in doing," Mara continued, "is assuming full responsibility for the upkeep, maintenance, and all of the other details of running a boat. Having a partner who could do those things would be the perfect solution for me."

She paused to let Alex absorb her words. Despite his initial reluctance and cautious response, he leaned forward and let her expand on the idea that was forming in her head even as she spoke.

"If, as you say, you've been longing for this seiner—and it sounds like you've checked it out thoroughly—then what I'm proposing is that I become a silent partner and that we each invest exactly 50 percent into the cost of the seiner. That will make us equal owners. You'll manage the full operation of the seiner, while I'll split full operating costs with you."

She watched Alex's body language and knew that his interest was piqued.

"We'll also share equally in all liabilities, losses and gains, and I will expect to be advised as to the status of the operation via a quarterly report. I think anyone would agree that that is only fair. You can use the extra money you have saved for your other needs."

Mara went inside for another cup of coffee, returning minutes later with one for both herself and for Alex. Around them, a light mist had begun to fall, making the hot beverage a welcome comfort.

"All of this, of course, will be spelled out in a business contract, which I would advise you to have your lawyer look over carefully before you commit."

Alex sipped his cup of hot coffee, apparently mulling the deal over in his head, while Mara pulled her sweater up close to her neck and slid her hands up into the sleeves for warmth. After a few minutes, she straightened herself, assuming a more businesslike pose.

"Lastly, Alex, should you decide to take advantage of my offer, I will only ask you to swear in writing that you will not reveal my identity to anyone outside your own banking and legal representatives, because you're soon going to learn that Jane is just a nickname I use to maintain my privacy."

"I don't know what to say Miss—"

"Just call me Jane for now, Alex. I'll talk to you more about this once you think it over and decide if you want to pursue this. In the meantime, I'll have my lawyer draw up a contract along with a background check on myself. I would only ask that you provide me with the same courtesy as far as a background check and credit report."

"Okay, Jane," Alex said cautiously. "Do you mind if I sleep on this?"

"Not at all," Mara answered. "I know this all seems impulsive to you, and the fact of the matter is that it is—but something tells me to do this, something deep inside, and so let's plan on meeting here on Friday with our lawyers and with an independent appraiser. If you decide not to take advantage of this offer, there's a good chance I'll just buy the seiner myself and look for someone to manage it for me. It's your opportunity for now, though, so give it some careful thought."

"I'll do that," Alex answered, getting up and walking to the door. "I'll definitely do that."

Chapter Ten
Storm Roamer

Doug Williams ran his hands along the bow of the *Driftfeather*. What a fine seiner she was.

"Can I help you?" a young man called down from the cabin door.

"I was just looking her over," Doug answered. "Saw the for sale sign. I didn't know anyone was here. Must've been you that just yanked it from the window."

"That it was. Name's Alex Winron."

Alex reached down to Doug, extending his hand.

"Doug Williams," Doug replied.

"I just closed the deal on buying the *Driftfeather* this morning," Alex said. "Sorry, but you're too late to buy this one."

"Not sure if I'm even looking," Doug answered. "Just here in town for the fisherman's lobby and thought I'd look around."

"Well, if you like what you see here, the *Driftfeather's* sister boat is across the bridge at the Douglas harbor. It's for sale, too. It's called *Storm Roamer.*"

"You don't say? Maybe I'll drive on over there and check her out."

"You won't be disappointed if you do," Alex answered. "If this deal didn't pan out, she was going to be my next choice. They're identical. Same upgrades, same everything but the paint color and the name. Only reason I chose this one is that things kind of fell into place for me on a good deal."

Alex Winron was as likable as any man Doug had ever met, and he was knowledgeable and keen about boats, too. He had tested him during their conversation and was sure of that. After chatting about some of the fine points of both seiners, he walked back along the docks and up to his truck, taking deep breaths of the familiar harbor scents that had long been such a major part of his life.

When he got to the Douglas harbor, he located the *Storm Roamer* at the far side of the harbor and looked her over just as he had started to do with the *Driftfeather*. Many of the fine points were the same, just as Alex had pointed out. The seiner appeared to be identical except that his one was painted dark green and the vessel's name was written in light blue on both sides of the bow and on the back panel right below the deck rail.

When he was finished looking things over, he stood on the dock staring at the letters that spelled out *Storm Roamer*. Suddenly a flood of memories of his lost seiner, the *Fire Ring Roamer* rushed into his mind. This was weird. He hadn't even seriously considered going back to sea just yet. It was almost as if something had led him to this place.

The seiner looked sound, and at 48 feet it was just the right length. The price was steep, but not for the quality it bought. For reasons he couldn't explain, he took a pen from his shirt pocket and jotted down the number listed on the *for sale* sign.

By the next morning, he had contacted the seller and made arrangements to thoroughly inspect all parts of the vessel. He even hired a diver to go into the water and look underneath.

The following day, he visited the bank and made arrangements for a loan, making a sizeable down payment with the insurance money he had received on the *Fire Ring Roamer*, money that Mara had refused to take her half of in their divorce. Using his last free afternoon in Juneau, he took the *Storm Roamer* over to Hoonah for a test run.

When he sailed past the last totem in the row that lined the beach on Graveyard Island just outside Hoonah, he was unable to avoid the sight of the tall totem with the large feather that ran up one side, and upon which a red dot was painted on the outer edge of the feather about a third of the way down. Suddenly he was shivering. He pulled the collar on his jacket up tightly around his neck, but it did little to help the intense shivering. Maybe he was coming down with something, but he had felt fine when he left.

It seemed like only yesterday, not two years ago, since the totem had been erected to honor a larger-than-life Native man named Joe Michael. Even now it was still a powerful connection to his life with Mara. The two of them had been there for the ceremony when it was erected. Shortly after that, they had gone to Sitka and gotten married. Now, just over one year since pledging to love each other forever—unbelievably—they were divorced.

Mara's face—smiling and beautiful—flashed into his consciousness, but despite his every attempt to keep it there, the image quickly faded. Then, just as quickly as it had begun, the shivering stopped. The warm feeling lingered, though, until long after he had sailed past the Hoonah harbor and was headed back to Juneau.

It had been a moment for sure—one in which, for the first time in a long while, everything felt right in this world. But his and Mara's life had not had the magical ending they had both foreseen on the beach that day when they honored Joe. He had probably just been caught up in the memory, so he stopped at the pharmacy on the way home and got a flu shot—just in case.

The next day, he phoned the seiner's owner and made arrangements to finalize the purchase, closing the deal later that week.

As the days went on, for whatever reason, he couldn't shake the memory of Hoonah. He wasn't sick and he knew it—unless being sick of aimless floundering counted. The traumas surrounding his brother's death and the loss of his first seiner were firmly part of the past, and the past was exactly where they should stay.

Now, with the purchase of the seiner, for the first time in a long time, Doug Williams felt like himself again. He was finally coming out of the black hole that he had fallen into. Suddenly he wanted to tell Mara. If ever he found her again he would. The chance was worth taking and he cast aside any thoughts of the possibility that she might not care. Life, it seemed, was finally returning to normal.

In two days, when the conference on fishing was over, he would set out on the *Storm Roamer* for Homer. In the meantime, he stocked up on supplies, making sure the title and permits were all in order. He left a message for Derrk Stanley, asking him to fly in from Homer to make the run back home with him. When Derrk called, he told him that he would pay him twice what he was making now just to get the man he wanted to make the trip. The two had worked well together for years, and it was time for them to do so again.

The old Doug Williams was back—the original version of the man he had been before circumstances beyond his control had derailed him. He stood there on the dock hardly able to contain his smile. Then he knocked on the wood of the *Storm Roamer's* side just for good measure, and just for his good luck to continue.

Chapter Eleven
Settling In

Now that it was winter, the days had shortened so much that everyone squinted on the rare days that the sun actually showed itself. Most days, though, it rained—except for the few when it snowed. There was no point in bemoaning the fact. Everyone was in the same situation.

Mara had firmed up her decision to not go back to the Juneau office of Ocean Research and Preserve. The friendly and supportive atmosphere she had enjoyed at the Homer office was definitely not evident in the Juneau office. After careful thought and consultation with her bosses back in Soldotna and Homer, she set up her own independent research company with one employee—herself. Any other assistance she needed would be contracted out on an as-needed basis. And so she began her new life in Juneau as a very private woman, who owned a business named So Biological, one half of a fishing seiner, a well-equipped inflatable boat, a cabin on pilings at the Juneau harbor, and who most everyone in town knew only as Jane.

Of course, Alex Winron knew who she was. She had shared that information with him early on, surprised when he revealed that he, too, was somewhat renowned. When he told her that he was the son of two Hollywood superstars, whose identity he swore her to protect, and whose trust fund he refused to tap into, Mara totally understood, just as she understood his wanting to prove to himself that he could be his own person.

It wasn't long before the two unlikely business partners became good friends, agreeing early on that their age difference was an instant deterrent to romance, and deciding that they would not consider themselves any more than friends—an agreement that took a lot of pressure and uncertainty away from their interactions and allowed them to form a solid friendship.

She told Alex about Brad and she told him about Doug, although not mentioning him by name. In return, Alex told her about becoming engaged once and, upon learning that his fiancée was cheating on him, had vowed to never become deeply involved with a show business woman again. In fact, he had sworn off women, he assured her—at least until the right one came along, if there really was such a thing as a "right one."

Mara met his parents, too, once when they came up to Juneau to see the seiner and after Alex had decided that she could be trusted knowing their identity. She joined the three of them and another couple who they described as close friends when they went down to Sitka for a few days.

She found them to be much different from their screen image and completely devoted to Alex, although to hear him talk one would have thought they were completely out of touch with the realities of everyday life. She enjoyed her time with them, and assured them that she would definitely call them the next time she found herself in the LA area or in Aspen, where they spent their winters.

After seeing them off, she flew back to Juneau, leaving Alex to hire a crew and prepare for the Sitka herring fishery, for which he had received a permit for this coming spring. Although he said he had the cash in hand, he had decided to finance $90,000 of the seiner—this despite her offer to carry the loan for him. Fortunately, the maneuver did not alter the previous owner's willingness to accept the reduced purchase price on the seiner.

"I want to build credit in my own name," Alex had told her. "For my whole life I've been living off my parents' money and now, in a way, yours. I want to build my own credit. I'll use the rest of the cash to get the seiner equipped and our business started up—like getting an inflatable boat for the seiner and having it equipped just like yours. Don't worry, I paid ahead on the first six payments with the money I saved partnering with you, so I won't feel any pressure financially or anything."

~ ~ ~

"Ain't seen you around much this winter," Stu said, as he leaned one elbow on the railing alongside the water and used his other hand to hold the cigar he was puffing on.

"I guess I've been keeping a low profile," Mara told him. "How have you been?"

Stu coughed, his face taking on a deep purplish red color as he gasped to recover, all the while trying to act like he was fine.

"Been alright. Been better and been worse, but still breathin' and that's what matters."

"You know, those stogies might not be the best thing for your cough, Stu."

"Yeah, I know what ya mean, young lady, and I'm gonna quit just as soon as I do, ya know?" Stu shrugged. "But until then, I'm choosin' to enjoy the only vice I got left to dally in, and if one day it kills me, then I guess one day I'll be dead."

She backed off, changing the subject.

"Otherwise you okay? Eating okay and sleeping okay and all that?"

"You bet I am. Sleep like a baby most every night—especially with the waves poundin' hard like they do in the winter. Why some mornings, I have to pinch myself to see if I'm still here," he said with a wink.

"Well, you let me know if the day comes when you're not," she laughed.

There was no sense trying to talk any sense into a man this set in his ways, and who looked to be well into his 70s and maybe even pushing 80.

"Alex is a good kid," Stu spurted out. "Ya made a good choice in puttin' him in charge of the seiner."

She stood dumbfounded as Stu pushed open the door to his cabin, walked inside, and clicked the latch behind him. How had Stu found out about Alex and the seiner?

Chapter Twelve
Questions

Alex denied having told anyone about their business arrangement when Mara emailed him that night. He swore he hadn't and shared her concern that word had somehow gotten out.

"Well, it's a small town for sure," she wrote back, speaking the words as she typed.

Alex wrote back about meeting the guy who bought the *Storm Roamer*, mentioning that he thought it was quite the coincidence that the sister ships had sat idle for two years and were now both back on the Alaska seas.

When he wrote that the new owner was a fisherman who lived in Homer, Doug's face flashed into her consciousness before the exchange shifted to the latest plans for this coming spring's Sitka herring fishery.

"We should meet up and talk about it soon," Mara wrote, and agreed to meet in person with him at her place the day after tomorrow at 9 a.m.

Later, while standing in line at the bank, she shifted uncomfortably when a familiar- looking man walked out to the window from a back room to answer a question from the clerk on duty. What was Lessis doing here? On closer inspection, she could see that his nametag read: K. Lessis, Branch Manager.

Interesting. Not only interesting, but enlightening. Was that how Stu had found out about her purchase of the seiner?

"Why, good morning Ms. Benson . . . er, I'm so sorry . . . most everyone here knows you as Jane, don't they?" Lessis said, feigning contriteness over violating her confidentiality.

"Good morning to you, Mr. Lessis. My but you seem to be a multifaceted presence in Juneau. Didn't I first meet you as one of the local police officials?"

"Now, now Ms. Ben . . . Jane," Lessis answered smugly. "I guess you hadn't heard the news that my wife's brother is president of this bank and needed somebody he felt was trustworthy to oversee things here in Juneau. There were some problems with the previous . . . Oh, let's not discuss that. I'm happy to report that I'm the new branch manager here, and please let me know if I can ever be of assistance to you or regarding any of your accounts."

Mara reluctantly shook Lessis's extended hand and forced herself to smile in spite of the misgivings she had about either the sincerity or helpfulness that he presented.

"And please call me Ken," he smiled without changing the impersonal expression in his eyes.

"Yes, of course. Thank you . . ."she let her voice fade as she looked uncomfortably around at who was watching. "Thank you, er, Ken."

Once finished with her banking and a few other errands, she returned to her cabin.

"Hi, Stu," she called to her elderly neighbor who was having a smoke out on his front deck.

"Jane!"

"I know about Lessis," she said flatly.

"Figured you'd find out soon enough," Stu answered, flicking his cigar into the harbor.

"That's environmentally bad, Stu," she admonished him.

"Yup. I suppose it is," Stu said, eyeing her squarely. "You enjoy the evening, now."

Stu wasn't one to keep chatting when he was done saying what he had to say. One day she'd press him for more on his relationship with Lessis, but for now she just nodded and watched him walk back inside.

Chapter Thirteen
Kona Coffee on the Deck

Heavy clouds hung low over Juneau as a light mist covered everything with the blanket of dampness that was the norm in Southeast Alaska.

Mara liked it. It made everything seem cozy. It also made the flower colors more vibrant, while accenting the shapes and forms of houses, boats, and other man-made things as if they had been strategically placed onto the hazy canvas of the earth like some type of human-generated art. No sunny day could be this beautiful, a reality lost on city dwellers surrounded by the blackness of wet pavement, and who often saw rain as nothing more than a depressing annoyance.

She went inside and poured some distilled water into the electric teapot, pressing the *on* button so that it would be ready the minute Alex arrived. When he got there minutes later, she put three scoops of espresso-grind Kona coffee into the double, brown filter paper-lined cone she had located after an intense Internet search and let the water trickle onto the dark powder, stirring it gently with the handle of a small brush as she watched the cups fill. Dancing amber beads forming on top of the brew assured her that the coffee was going to taste just right.

Some might consider it pretentious to carry the genuine crystal mugs outside onto the deck table, but crystal enhanced the aroma and the taste of the coffee, a fact she had learned years ago. It was impossible to find real crystal coffee mugs anymore, but it was worth the risk of breaking one to actually use the ones she had. Brad had taught her the pleasure of indulging in a perfect cup of coffee—the drinking of which was as much an experience as it was the enjoying of a beverage.

She had left the deck umbrella closed, too. The mist was fine and she wanted to savor it. A zip-up wool sweater, jeans, knee-high rubber boots that were regulation wear for the area, and a tight-fitting wool cap would keep her toasty and warm while they sat outside. Dressed similarly, Alex sat down at the table across from her.

"I've got the report from last quarter here for you," he said. "You can see that there's some pretty hefty maintenance expenses this time, but I felt I should have everything gone over thoroughly at least once before we put the *Driftfeather* out to work. I also paid another six months ahead on my loan since I don't want to forget any payments while I'm out working."

"I think that was a wise decision, Alex."

Like her, Alex didn't believe in automatic withdrawal of payments from his savings account and preferred to personally make his payments at the bank.

"I was right there during the whole inspection," Alex said. "There's nothing on that seiner I don't understand."

Mara smiled and took a sip of her coffee, holding the crystal mug cupped in her hands. Alex had turned out to be the perfect business partner. Each time they talked, she realized it more and more. Even his reports were neatly written. Analytical, organized, mostly computer generated, but with a fair sprinkling of handwritten detail added in black ink, with a penmanship that was articulately rendered in a way that reminded her of timeless ancient ship's logs.

"I want to wax the instrument panel and detail the upholstery inside," he continued. "Maybe by Thursday you'd like to join me for a run over to Hoonah—just to test her out," he said.

As she nodded in agreement, he added, "I thought maybe we could invite old Stu along for the ride. Give him a chance to get out to sea again."

It was a fine idea. She would let Alex invite Stu man to man, knowing that Stu would be more likely to accept if he felt he was needed on the trip.

"The truth is, I'd value his opinion of the *Driftfeather's* fitness before we really put her to work," Alex said.

"Then let's do it," she agreed. "I'll pick up supplies and food this afternoon."

"I think you're doing a great job, Alex," she added.

He didn't let her see one corner of his mouth turn upward in a half smile as he carried the crystal mugs back inside.

"I told you I wouldn't let you down, Mara," he said, using her real name, which he rarely did.

"I've got a date with someone other than the *Driftfeather* for a change tonight," he laughed, "so if you don't mind, I think I'll take the rest of the day off."

"I just hope she's not one of your Hollywood friends," Mara teased him.

"She's not," he said, a tad embarrassed at having even revealed her existence.

"I was just teasing, Alex. I hope you both have a wonderful time."

"Thanks," he answered sheepishly.

She sat staring at the door for several minutes after he left. The fact that he had told her about this date told her it was serious. Alex was not a player—at least not from what she had observed. If he was about to find that someone special, no one could be happier for him than she was. Love really was grand when you found it, which made losing it hurt all the more.

Busying herself with washing the crystal mugs and straightening up her cabin, she started a list of things she would need to pick up for the trip to Hoonah on Thursday.

Chapter Fourteen
Maiden Voyage

Thursday's weather was a repeat of Wednesday's, Tuesday's, Monday's, and all the days as far back as recent memory would allow. As a matter of fact, the last time anyone could remember seeing the sun had been at least two months ago—a day so fine that nearly the entire population of Juneau had found some reason to either call in sick or leave work early just to savor the experience.

Mara threw her duffel bag onto the cart that Stu was pushing toward the dock. Soon, Alex would hoist it onto the seiner using the public winches, along with a couple of crab pots that he would set out along the way.

"Packed kinda heavy, young lady," Stu said matter-of-factly.

She raised her eyebrows and glanced at him, saying nothing.

By 10 a.m. they were moving out of the Juneau harbor with both Mara and Alex surprised to see the *Storm Roamer* moving out right ahead of them.

"This is the *Driftfeather* asking if all's clear up ahead, *Storm Roamer*?" Alex spoke into the mike.

"This is the *Storm Roamer* reporting clear sailing ahead," a male voice boomed back.

"All's well to the rear," Alex said back into the mike, before sitting back in the captain's chair to guide the *Driftfeather* out of the harbor.

The voice from the *Storm Roamer* had sounded familiar. It wasn't Derrk Stanley's, was it?

"Alex, do you know the skipper of the *Storm Roamer*?" Mara asked.

"I met the new owner. Sorry I can't remember his name. Said he was from Homer, though. The skipper's a guy named Doug or Todd or something like that . . ."

Alex turned his attention back to steering the seiner north, while Mara watched as the *Storm Roamer* moved in the opposite direction.

"You look like you've seen a ghost, Jane," Stu said, snapping her out of deep thought.

"Could be that I have, Stu. Could be that I have."

While Alex and Stu sat up on the bridge discussing the fine points of navigation, she put the groceries away and prepared sandwiches for lunch. Could it possibly be Doug Williams who had bought her seiner's sister ship? She tried to quell the recurrent thought.

"Looks like we got us some ice coming up!" Stu bellowed from the bridge.

"Whoa! And looks like we got us about three orcas right off the starboard bow," he bellowed again.

Mara ran to the right side of the seiner just in time to see not just three, but six orcas swimming right beside the *Driftfeather*. For several seconds, they swam along with the seiner, the tall dorsal fins of the two males moving steadily with four females alongside. The sight of them was exhilarating.

"They're transients," Stu said knowingly.

Somehow he knew how to tell the more predatory variety of killer whales from their less aggressive local counterparts. Sure enough, as they passed several icebergs, one of the whales rose up and snatched a seal that had not yet reached the ice.

"It's nature," Stu said when Mara turned away from the grisly sight. "It's survival. It's the food chain."

"Seems like a good time for lunch," Alex called out, instantly realizing the irony of his words.

Slowing the seiner to a crawl, they bobbed in the flat seas fighting off seagulls as they ate, and thinking that maybe the dots out beyond were possibly some Dall porpoise. By the time they could see Graveyard Island off in the distance, it was late afternoon.

"I've gotta catch a few z's," Stu said, abruptly heading to the sleeping area below.

When Mara went to wake him up later, Stu was sitting on a bunk, leaning with his back against the wall, reading a book.

Chapter Fifteen
What's with Stu?

What was the deal with Stu? The way he had retreated, it was almost as if he wanted to avoid all things Hoonah. Maybe he had felt some of the same trepidation that Mara had when the *Driftfeather* had approached Graveyard Island. The encounter had turned out to be uneventful, though, and Joe Michael's totem, which had once loomed so strongly in the foreground of her impression of the remote island, now seemed to blend in with the others—dulled, weathered, faded—nothing to mark it as any different from all the rest. Even the feather Joe Michael had given her stayed in her bag, where she had stuffed it down tightly near the bottom after finding it lying on the floor of the wheelhouse.

She watched as Alex slowed and steered into the harbor as much for a test of the maneuverability of the *Driftfeather* as for a break before heading back to Juneau. Stu, for whatever reason, remained sequestered in the cabin. Whatever his issue with Hoonah was, it would have to be his own little secret for now.

Of more concern—well, not so much of concern, but more of curiosity—was the fact that Derrk Stanley, or someone that could be his voice double, was radioing from the *Storm Roamer*, and that the *Driftfeather's* sister ship had been purchased by someone from Homer.

Was it possible that Doug Williams was going back out to sea? If so, the *Storm Roamer* would be a logical choice, both because of its name being so similar to his beloved *Fire Ring Roamer* and because Doug knew a good-quality seiner when he saw one. She had been with Doug long enough to know that both the *Driftfeather* and the *Storm Roamer* had all the characteristics and qualities that he would have been looking for in a seiner, that is, *if* he had been looking for a seiner, which she found hard to believe.

On the other hand, just why was it that she was this curious about the activities of the man she had recently divorced? Hadn't she moved beyond any feelings she had for him or his lifestyle? She shrugged her shoulders as she tried to dismiss the intrusive thoughts, forcing her mind to think about things like the research paper she needed to finish by this time next week, but thoughts of Doug kept creeping into her mind.

Nothing is ever going to make me go back to him, she told herself. *Nothing, that is, if he even had any inclination to try to win her back, and who said that he did? Stop it, Mara! How dumb are you, anyway? Stop thinking about this! You're letting your mind run away with itself. Get a grip, woman!* But no thoughts could quell the questions rampaging through her curious mind.

The sound of Alex's voice finally forced a break in the anxiety-laden train of thought.

"I'm thinkin' she did pretty good, Mara. You?"

"Uh, yeah, I guess so—yes. Yes, Alex, she did very well and so did you. I was very impressed with the way she traveled, maneuvered—all of it. Yes, absolutely I am pleased."

Why was she acting this way—so anxious and so unsettled?

"I see that the *Storm Roamer* also has a permit for the Sitka herring fishery," Alex said absently. "I'm thinking of looking up the new owner and seeing about teaming up."

"I don't know, Alex. Why would you want to do that?"

She didn't wait for him to answer before busying herself in the galley. She hadn't prepared herself for dealing with anything like this. Joe Michael's words popped into her head—the same words he had used when handing her the feather on the car deck of the Alaska State ferry two years ago:

Your present is
the future of your past.
All who come here
seek the future
of their past.
You will need this
to protect . . .

She slammed her mind shut on the rest. She didn't even have the original feather Joe had given her anymore. She had given it to Della right after drug cartel kingpin, Carlos Antoya, had shot the young woman last year in Glenallen, leaving her with her right arm still in need of several more surgeries.

As far as she knew, the feather and its purported powers of protection now resided with Della. Besides, she didn't need any protection from Doug Williams even if he had, in fact, purchased the *Storm Roamer*.

"Do what you think is best, Alex. I'm not even sure I'll be able to go out with you to Sitka," she said, knowing all the while that she would be there if she wanted to, no matter how worried she felt about running into Doug Williams again.

"I'll draw up some proposed approaches to getting the most out of our permit," Alex answered. "Maybe we can talk more later."

"Yes," Mara answered simply. "Later . . ."

Chapter Sixteen
Old Ways

It wasn't until later in the evening after returning from Hoonah that Alex noticed that the expense logbook for the *Driftfeather* had been moved. Normally he kept it with his maps and other necessary papers in a special slot to the left of the wheel on the bridge. That's exactly where he found it, except that the latest receipts he had left tucked inside where now stuffed into the slot beside it, and it was inserted spiral end inward into its slot, rather than the other way around as was the norm.

Maybe Mara had looked it over when he had given her the wheel while he took a break to use the head and then put his feet up for thirty minutes to relax on the way to Hoonah.

"I didn't even know you kept it in there," she told him when he stopped by to ask her about it on his way home that night. "Come to think of it, though, I did see Stu fiddling with his vest right after you left, but I was too busy minding the wheel to really pay him much mind. Anyway, he went down for his nap right about then, so now I really wonder—especially since I found him sitting up in his berth when I checked on him later."

"Why would Stu . . ." Alex let his voice trail off. "Since the account number and our password was on the inside cover, I'll check with the bank in the morning and make sure everything is okay."

"I can't imagine that Stu—" Mara began.

"Me either," Alex said, not letting her finish. "If anything, it was probably just harmless curiosity, especially with Stu having been a boat owner himself. Maybe he was just curious about today's costs and all. I should never have left the log out like that anyway. I had planned on bringing it inside tonight, but just hadn't done it yet."

"Why would you normally be in any rush?" She said, mostly to reassure Alex. "You hadn't brought on anyone but your partner and a friend so far."

Secretly, though, she felt the error had the potential to be serious and hoped with all her might that it wasn't.

~~~

Alex had already checked with the bank and knew that everything was in order when he asked Stu about the logbook the next day. Just to be safe, he had already changed the password to the account.

Stu's demeanor was humble and apologetic.

"I ain't gonna lie to ya, kid," Stu told him. "When you went down to the head and your sidekick, Jane here, ran to the galley to grab a cold drink, the logbook fell on the floor and so I picked 'er up. There was loose papers layin' everywhere and so I opened it up to stuff 'em back inside and saw that the book was your financial accountin' for the *Driftfeather*.

"I can't deny that curiosity got the better of me and I started readin' to see how today's prices compared to when I skippered my own seiner, and so I tucked it under my vest and took it down to my berth to read and tucked it back in your slot once we were docked back in Juneau, figurin' that no one would ever know the difference."

Alex stared at Stu, stifling any anger at what were apparently the harmless curiosities of an old man, while Stu lit up one of his stogies and looked down over his railing at an otter swimming on its back in the water right below. A few feet farther out sat the first of the large row of fishing boats that made their permanent home in the Juneau harbor.

"Costs a damn sight more today then it did in my day," Stu laughed, trying to lighten the mood. "I can tell you for sure that I'm glad it ain't me havin' to pay out that kinda money anymore."

"Yeah, I guess you have a pretty good perspective from where you sit, Stu," Alex answered. "Since no harm's done and you've been man enough to be honest with me, I'll consider it resolved, and I'll learn from this and keep the book in a secure location so that no one's tempted to get into it again."

"I appreciate yer understandin'," Stu said, flicking his stogie into the water.

"Stu, can I set you up with an ash can or something?" Alex asked.

"Oh, sorry, kid. You talkin' about the stogie? Yer sidekick, Jane's, been getting' on me about that lately, too. It's all natural, ya know, but since it seems to be upsettin' everyone, I guess I'll just try not to do it anymore."
~~~

"Well, smoking's not good for anyone's health, Stu, but I don't want to try to tell you what to do. Sorry, I mentioned it. It's really none of my business if you choose to smoke . . ."

Alex shifted uncomfortably. The conversation with Stu had already been difficult. How often does a person have to confront a friend and neighbor about something as sensitive as accessing confidential material? Hadn't Stu helped him with many of the technicalities of learning about seiners? Now here he was, making an old man feel uncomfortable by displaying youthful paranoia about money, smoking, and just about everything else that came out of his mouth today.

Maybe he should just leave—take a couple of days off and regroup. Maybe some of the realities of owning the seiner were catching up with him. Was he really experienced enough to handle such a big undertaking? Had he overestimated his ability in thinking he could learn the ropes from the inside out? Handle this kind of job? People had to be wondering just what kind of businessman he was to leave confidential information lying around anyway? Was he in over his head with this whole endeavor?

Tomorrow he would talk with Mara about hiring a bookkeeper. It would reinforce her trust in him if he showed he was serious about not making any more stupid mistakes. He felt the tightness go out of his shoulders at the decision. Better to have a neutral third party expert manage the books. Running the seiner and fishing would be enough challenge in themselves. Besides, his mission was clear, and the seiner was a big part of the undertaking he had begun since arriving in Juneau.

"Guess I ain't good fer much anymore in this world. Old and nosy, and now pollutin' the very ocean that sustained my livelihood," Stu said, pulling Alex's thoughts back to the present.

Wishing this conversation had never been necessary, Alex stared at his feet.

"Come on now, Stu, if those stogies haven't killed you by now, then chances are you're good. I'm sorry I mentioned it."

"Well, won't be that many more years that I'll be imprintin' my ways on this here earth, so worry not, kid. Sorry. Sorry about all of it," Stu finished, making Alex feel worse than he already did, if that was even possible.

He watched Stu walk into his tiny cabin and close the door. The sound of the deadbolt sliding closed snapped in the cold air. For a minute he stood there, staring at the water where Stu's stogie was still floating below the dock. The otter dove, coming up a few minutes later under the soggy glob, before diving again and disappearing from view.

Chapter Seventeen
Dinner for . . .?

Mara assured Alex that hiring a bookkeeper would be a relief to both of them and gave him a week to look around and find someone he thought he could work with. At his suggestion, she would meet with them, too, but the choosing, she reminded him, would be up to him, because he was the one essentially running the show.

The moment she knew would one day arrive came much earlier than expected when she ran into Doug at the grocery store that afternoon.

"Mara," he said as he pushed his cart toward her, "I can't believe it's you."

"Doug?" she answered, feeling the muscles in her shoulders tighten uncomfortably.

"I heard you might be in Juneau. I can't believe I found you."

She pushed her cart around to the next aisle and continued shopping, but Doug followed right behind.

"Mara, we need to talk."

"What could we have to talk about anymore, Doug?" she said icily, but inside she sensed something different about Doug. He seemed more like he had been when she first met him—confident, centered, balanced. "Besides, I'm in a hurry."

"There's a café over near the Baranof Hotel where I'm staying and there's also a great restaurant. I'm only here for another couple of days until the fisherman's lobby is over and then I'll be heading back to Homer. I could meet you there later. We could talk over dinner."

"Are you going to bring your girlfriend?" She sniped.

Ignoring the jab, he said, "I'll be there waiting in the dining room at seven—alone—since they won't let my usual dinner partner, Thor, inside."

Mara watched him push his cart to the check stand and pay for the few items he had picked up, and then she looked down, refusing to look at him anymore. How dare he act so nonchalant, or even have the gall to assume she wanted to talk to him, much less have dinner with him?

She made several other stops, including one to thank the manager at the boat store for all his help with the inflatable.

"I just love it," she told him. "I've had it out several times and it's perfect for what I need."

She also stopped to upgrade her cell phone to a satellite phone that included a GPS. Although more expensive, its practical value would far outweigh the increased cost. If she were going to be out on the water, she would need reliable communication.

On the advice of the boat store manager, she also purchased a locator beacon.

"It's not good to be out in remote areas alone, even if you're just skimming the shoreline in your boat, but if that's what you intend to do, then at least use common sense and make sure someone can find you if you get in trouble."

Once back inside her cabin, she put everything away and threw a log into the woodstove to take the chill off the room.

To say it had been a shock to run into Doug was an understatement. Strange how he had acted so laid-back after everything that had happened between them. Was he really that shallow?

She made herself a cup of tea and propped her feet up in front of the woodstove, stooping to pick up the latest feather from Joe Michael that had fallen to the floor. Suddenly, for some unknown reason, she jumped up and took a quick shower before putting on a clean pair of jeans over which she pulled on the new boiled-wool sweater she had purchased last week.

Kicking her Uniroyals off to the side, she pulled on the tall fur-lined leather boots she had picked up in Anchorage before she left, wrapped a long wool scarf whose ends fell well below her knees around her neck, and started walking the few blocks to the Baranof Hotel.

By the time she got there, the humidity had caused her long hair to spring into the usual wild curls that defied any attempt to control them. Pulling the mane back from her face, she arranged it in a loose ponytail and secured it with one of the scrunchies that she always carried with her. The several wisps of hair that she couldn't corral fell loosely around her face, where they would just have to stay.

"Mara," Doug called, standing up from a table along the wall in the dining room. "I didn't think you would come."

Chapter Eighteen
Fine Dining

While Doug pulled a chair out so she could sit down, a rapid-fire array of thoughts that included bolting from the room ran through Mara's head. What was she even doing here? Suddenly, a disturbance near the entry disrupted the tranquility of the dining room. Before she could sit down, a dog came bounding through the restaurant, knocking over a tray being carried to a table by a server, and narrowly missing two others who rushed to help.

Next thing she knew, Thor had his front paws on her shoulders and was licking her face like there was no tomorrow.

"Thor! Thor!" she called, hoping he would sit or stay or do something besides nearly knock her backwards off her chair.

"Thor!" Doug hissed, and the dog looked briefly toward his owner before again nuzzling her with his head.

"Sir. Madam. There are absolutely no animals allowed inside the hotel," the maitre'd said firmly.

Doug stood and grabbed a hold of Thor's collar while she stood to regain her composure. Unfortunately, Thor broke loose from Doug and once again proceeded to jump on her, pulling the tablecloth off the table, along with four place settings of fine china, silver, and crystal. In the clamor that followed, one of the broken pieces tore a long gash in the antique wallpaper that was a hallmark of the establishment, and an entire bottle of wine soaked into the carpet leaving giant purple splotches extending several feet out from the table.

Somehow, against all odds, she managed to get Thor under control and lead him outside while Doug stayed behind to try to make arrangements to settle the damages.

She was standing a few feet from the door when a patrol car pulled up and a uniformed officer approached her and asked to see her ID as well as Thor's tags.

Thankfully, Doug had remembered to get Thor his new license at the beginning of the year, which also indicated that his rabies vaccination was current.

"You do realize there is a leash law in Juneau, miss, don't you?" the officer asked her, making his words sound more like a statement than a question.

Mara apologized and explained that Thor had been securely shut inside their boat and must have somehow gotten loose.

"My husband is inside trying to settle any damages right now," she said, fudging the truth.

After asking her to wait where she was, the officer went inside, returning a few minutes later to tell her that the damages had been settled and she was free to go.

By the time Doug came out, she was sitting on a bench outside the restaurant and Thor was lying asleep beside her on the bench with his head in her lap.

"Mara," Doug said, looking exhausted and embarrassed.

But before he could say anymore, she began to laugh and suddenly Doug was laughing, too.

"Talk about breaking the ice. Are you okay, Mara? It looks like he put a few snags in your sweater."

"He just saved me the trouble of breaking it in."

"Look, I know you have every reason to go running away right now," Doug said, his tone suddenly serious, "but if you'll give me a few minutes, I'll take Thor back to my boat . . ."

"Better yet, why don't I just walk there with you," she answered. "I'll be able to find my way back okay."

Chapter Nineteen
Uncharted Waters

Mara knew her way around any set of docks in Alaska. Her days on the run from Carlos Antoya and his thugs had taken her to most of them, some more than once. It was almost an anticlimax, then, when the boat Doug led her to ended up being the *Storm Roamer*, which he had apparently moved from the Douglas harbor over to the Juneau side.

"Somehow I knew it was Derrk Stanley's voice I heard over the radio a week ago," she said simply.

"It's true that Derrk is helping me with the boat," Doug said, "but we've only been out once on a short run to Hoonah."

"The *Driftfeather*'s my boat," she answered. "It belongs to me and my business partner, a young man named Alex Winron. We were right behind you on that day, but slowed to look at some orcas that were putting on quite a show."

"This is incredible," Doug said, hoisting Thor up onto the deck of the *Roamer*. "I saw the orcas, too, but Derrk and I were focusing on testing the seiner before I bought it and so we kept going. I was just here in town like I am every year and I ran into this kid, Alex as you call him, and next thing I know, I'm buying another seiner—and a really nice one at that."

Suddenly Mara was exhausted.

"I think I've reached my limit on surprises for this day," she said, picking up her jacket and straightening her clothes. "Thanks, anyway, for the almost dinner."

Turning, she started walking away from Doug and his boat. When she got around the first turn to the long dock and right before she began the steep climb up the floating stairs, she turned and looked back to find him sitting on the deck watching her with his arm around Thor's neck.

When she did, Doug waved and Thor woofed, but neither tried to stop her and for that she was grateful.

When she got back to her cabin, the fire was all but out in the woodstove, so she threw a log in and then another for good measure before noticing that the feather was on the floor again.

Making a mental note to find somewhere secure to keep it from falling victim to the drafts that seemed to be blowing it off the table all the time, she tucked it into a book she had been reading, before changing into her nightshirt and climbing into bed for the night.

Just to be safe, she checked to see if her 9mm was in the nightstand where she normally kept it. Somehow, knowing she had the gun made her feel less vulnerable.

Chapter Twenty
Misty Solace

Mara savored the privacy of sitting on her deck the next morning. It was late in February and the foggy seclusion felt comforting. Things were quiet around town with many having gone off on vacation to places like Hawaii, Belize, or southern Mexico to escape the Alaska winter's cold and darkness. In the distance, a couple of boats knocked against the docks and something clanged rhythmically in time, creating an eerie symphony with the gently lapping waves underneath her cabin.

Just a few months earlier, she had made a dramatic exit from everything and everyone she knew, even getting rid of her almost new SUV. Last night, unbelievably, she had laughed with the very man she had then sworn to have nothing to do with again. Not only laughed, but had followed him home without as much as a thought to the past.

Where was her newfound independence, not to mention her steely resolve to begin anew? Apparently she was as fickle as he was—and as impulsive.

She went inside and made herself another cup of Kona, this time pouring it into one of the travel mugs she kept on hand. Grabbing her Gortex jacket, she pulled on her Uniroyals and climbed down through the trap door in the deck to her dinghy.

Halfway down the ladder made of wooden slats nailed to one of the dock's support pilings, she punched in the code to the keyless entry and opened the waterproof box that someone had built there long ago, retrieving her lifejacket, emergency kit, and repair kit, which she threw down into her raft below. She then locked her house keys inside the box and climbed the rest of the way down.

She was glad she had remembered to bring mittens as the winter air sent a chill through her that went right to the bone. Right now she relished the feeling, though, as well as the solitude as she putted in the dinghy along the shoreline for several miles. The sun had not yet risen, but there was just enough light from the full moon and the breaking dawn to see her way.

When she saw a couple of wolves walking along the water's edge, she chastised herself for forgetting her shotgun, but feeling no real danger, watched them on their morning hunt, all the while enjoying the privilege of the rare sight from her vantage point safely inside the inflatable boat.

She loved the spruce forests, shrouded as they were in this misty aura of aloneness. Was there any more peaceful place on this earth than right here? Beside her, two otters rolled lazily on their backs, using small stones to pound open the shells that they held on their chests as a couple of seagulls hovered above, ready to take advantage of any lost parts of the otter's tasty meal.

In the distance, a seal popped its head out of the water; its huge welcoming eyes making contact with hers as if watching her every move. It soon disappeared into the water only to surface minutes later, hundreds of feet away, but still watching her.

The sound of an eagle's screech pierced the air, followed by several more. Within minutes, several of the majestic birds had swooped down close to the water, their white heads and tails reflecting the glimmering orange glow of the rising sun. One of them succeeded in snatching a fish out of the rolling sea and then quickly flew off across the water with the other eagles tailing right behind. Once on shore, they would jockey for the best position from which to snatch the prized catch should the lucky eagle let down his guard for even a moment.

The raft motor sputtered a bit, causing her to have to adjust the throttle to keep it running, but the situation was momentary. Still, perhaps it was time to turn around and go back home. She made a mental note to pick up a gas can to carry in the raft in case she lost track of time next time out and traveled too far. Although she had oars, she would much prefer to use the motor.

On her way into the harbor, she passed the *Storm Roamer*. She could see Doug and Derrk working on the deck, but she didn't notice Thor until he raised his head from the bench he had been lying on to watch her go by.

Luckily, the men didn't see her, nor did they react to Thor's succession of three barks before he lay back down again.

Any answers to the mystery behind the failing of their relationship that Doug had been willing to provide during their ill-fated dinner would have to go unanswered for now. Still, for the first time in a long time, she felt a tiny spark inside the heart she had forced to stop feeling, before she made herself stop thinking his name, tied up her dinghy, retrieved her house key from the lockbox, stuffed the life preserver, emergency kit and repair kit back inside, and climbed back up the ladder to her cabin.

Chapter Twenty-One
Wedding Bells and the Rain

Alex had been working furiously to ready the *Driftfeather* for its first major outing under his ownership. He had made a decision not to partner with the *Storm Roamer* as soon as he learned that Doug Williams was the ex-husband Mara had referred to when they met.

It wasn't that he had anything against Williams; it was just that he felt the potential for conflict of interest was too high, and it was important that Mara did not question his loyalty. Still, he remained on friendly terms with Doug Williams, and the two agreed that they would engage in friendly competition for the prized herring roe of the Sitka sac roe herring fishery in March.

As it turned out, the plan was one that served them well as both he and Doug Williams exceeded their expectations and enjoyed a lucrative first outing of the season. Lucrative enough for Alex to inform Mara that he had just proposed to his girlfriend, Emily, who he had first introduced to her just before leaving for Sitka.

The wedding was held in Juneau in late April and a small reception followed at the same hotel where Thor had unceremoniously jeopardized any chance that either Mara or Doug would be welcome there again. But no one turned either of them away the evening of the gathering, much to their surprise.

Fortunately for Mara, Emily had arranged for her to be seated at a table across the room from Doug, which made for a comfortable evening—that is, until he cornered her for a dance after, which he led her outside for a walk around the docks.

Perhaps it was the wine, or maybe just the joy of the occasion, but she let him guide her along the waterfront in the light rain that was the norm for this time of year.

"Nothing happened between Erin and me," he told her, filling her in on the details of how Erin had lost the baby she had been determined to carry and had leaned on him for support.

"She had lost her mother, her friend, Ethan, and become pregnant by the man who had killed her mother. I don't have to tell you the story, because you were there, living it with me the whole way," he said.

She wanted to leave—run, even, from the discussion, but she stayed knowing it was one that needed to take place.

"You and I had already filed for divorce. Look, Mara, I'm not saying that what was going on wasn't on the verge of moving into dangerous waters, but the point is—thanks to Ben and the others—the point is that I came to my senses and saw things for what they were and ended it."

She felt her eyes fill with tears, not sure if they were tears of anger, hurt, or just relief at having the truth come out.

"Erin was—is—the spitting image of her mother," Doug said. "I suppose that part of me wanted to bring Sassy back, maybe even find a way to make up for any hurt I caused her . . .

"I don't know. It was such a confusing time for me. With everything that was going on then, I guess I just fell into this hole I couldn't climb out of and it all came to a head with our divorce. The Erin thing, well, it was just a sideshow to what was really going on inside me."

Mara forced herself to stay calm, even as her mind raced with torrents of words she wanted to hurl Doug's way. Why was he telling her all this? Was he trying to ease his own conscience? Did he think she would just accept it and pretend it never happened? Finally, in words that surprised even her, she spoke.

"Alex says that he's taking the *Driftfeather* out into the Gulf next week and that you're going to fish there, too, before heading back to Homer."

Doug nodded as they continued walking.

"I was just thinking that if you wanted to leave Thor with me, it would be good to have him with me again."

"He'd love that, Mara, and I'd love that."

He placed his arm lightly around her waist and she let him. Then he walked her back to the reception, thanked Alex for including him in the wonderful evening, kissed her lightly on the cheek, and walked alone in the rain back to the *Storm Roame*r.

Chapter Twenty-Two
What the . . .

Since Alex and Emily would be out fishing for several months, Mara had agreed to collect their mail and take care of any outstanding bills that might arise.

Marriage had not changed Alex's business practices and he continued to refuse to pay online, so that left Mara on shore to take care of any additional business in person. Alex had already made payments on what he owed on the *Driftfeather* well into the next year, so when she got a notice, followed a month later by another notice saying that payments were overdue, she was forced to contact him at sea.

"Everything's paid up," Alex told her. "It has to be a mistake."

After giving her his pin number and other identifying information, and wiring his consent for her to access his account at the bank, she made an appointment and went in to see what was amiss.

Because she was a silent partner and her portion of the money had been placed on the boat by Alex, there was no link between her personal account and the *Driftfeather* account—a measure that her lawyer had set up to protect her assets. Neither did her name appear on the title of the seiner, although legal documents defined hers and Alex's business relationship and the fact that upon any sale or loss of the seiner, he would owe her half its purchase price.

"It looks like your little business friend took advantage of your good nature, Ms. Benson, and failed to uphold his part of the purchase of the *Driftfeather*," Lessis said, peering over his glasses as he turned the documents outlining Alex's payments for her to see.

Lessis's sleazy innuendo was nearly as offensive as the cheap cologne he seemed to like to slather on for his new role as a bank official. His choice of a dark blue overly shiny suit as business attire only added to the image of slovenly tastelessness with which he presented himself.

"I'm not sure I see the problem here," Mara said evenly, pointing to Alex's two pre-payments that each covered a span of six months, and trying to ignore the fact that Lessis had gathered too much information about hers and Alex's business dealings.

"I can see why you're unable to grasp the issue," Lessis said, leaning in a little too much.

She bristled at the condescending tone of both his words and demeanor.

"If you will look here, you'll see that for every payment he submitted, a subsequent withdrawal of 50 percent—sometimes 75 percent—was made from the account over several weeks after each deposit."

"Mr. Winron assures me that he made no such withdrawals. Is it not possible that the bank could have made an error?" She asked him.

"That is very unlikely, Ms. Benson. Our tellers are of the highest caliber and operate with flawless efficiency. Why, if you'll look here, many of these transactions were handled by me or by my assistant manager, and I assume you are not intending to question the integrity of a former law enforcement professional."

Lessis stared at her for an uncomfortably long time before adding, "Then again, Ms. Benson, you seem to have all the information necessary to access the account."

Mara's scathing look stopped Lessis from expanding on his inference.

"Nonetheless, Mr. Lessis," she said evenly, "I would like to request a copy of the payment history on this account so that I can compare it to the receipts Mr. Winron received for the transactions."

"Well . . . it appears you have the proper authorization to access this information, so if you'll give me a moment, I'll prepare a statement for you."

"Thank you," Mara answered, before walking across the bank lobby to take a seat on a bench by the door.

Something fishy was going on here. Hopefully, it would all amount to just a simple clerical error. The trouble was, she was going to have to try to reach Alex again to find out where he kept the receipts, and that was going to be a problem since he had already told her he would be out of range for the next week and unable to be reached except by emergency relay through the Coast Guard.

"Are you aware that Mr. Winron has received his second to the last foreclosure notice, Ms. Benson?" Lessis said, returning with the printed payment history.

"Foreclosure?" she said, looking him directly in the eye. "Foreclosure on what?"

"Foreclosure on the *Driftfeather*," Lessis smirked. "Too bad to lose such a fine seiner, too, not to mention the damage that this will inflict on his credit rating."

"Then let us avert any such potential, Mr. Lessis," she told him after glancing at the statement. "I will have the $17,035.07 that you say Alex is past due transferred into his account by no later than 3 p.m.today. Meanwhile, I *will* get to the bottom of what happened here, but it may take me into the week after next to accomplish it."

"Very well, Ms. Benson. If either Smith Bank or I can be of further assistance to you, please . . ."

"Good day, Mr. Lessis. I'll keep that in mind."

Chapter Twenty-Three
Hmm . . .

By late that afternoon, Mara had loaded the dinghy, this time remembering to bring the shotgun in its waterproof case. Now that Thor was with her, she continued to climb down to the raft in the usual way, and then maneuver around to the bottom of the floating steps to let him run down the ramp from the dock that held her row of cottages to get in. The tide was almost out and Thor hesitated slightly before inching his way down the steep ramp to her.

"Ain't heard any barkin', so guess I didn't know ya had a dog," Stu called down from the railing outside his cabin, just narrowly missing her boat with the stump of stogie he threw down.

"I haven't seen much of you lately, Stu," she called up. "I see you haven't managed to get yourself an ashtray yet."

"Look here now, missy, this ain't the South-48 where we got all those hi-falutin' rules. If ya want to be an Alaskan, yer gonna have to learn to deal with real men and real life."

What was with Stu, anyway? He was usually cranky, but never this much so. Not really in the mood to deal with him or his mood right now, she backed the raft away from the steps and slowly turned it around.

"I'm just going north along the shore," she called to him. "I should be back around dark."

The fact of the matter was that it was long past dark when she finally returned. There had been no reason for the delay other than her desire to enjoy every possible second that the time away from all things human could provide.

She had been surprised by how much Thor enjoyed the raft with her, usually lying on the soft bottom, but sometimes standing with his front paws on one of the wood seats to scan the shoreline, once even letting out a low growl when something moved in the brush—something that turned out to be a black bear moving along the shoreline.

But solitude had its limits and this time the limit was the fact that she was nearly out of gas in spite of the two extra gallons she had brought along. Tomorrow she would look into a bigger motor, or maybe even a second motor if the inflatable could handle the weight. As much as she liked her new dinghy, what she had learned was that she wanted broader range with it, and so she would have it adapted to better suit her needs.

When she dropped Thor off at the dock, Stu was standing in front of her cabin with his hand on the doorknob. Startled, he quickly withdrew it and walked briskly to his own door.

"Well, finally gettin' back, I see," he called to her. "I was just checkin' to make sure your door was secure before I went to bed."

"Thanks, Stu," she called to him as she maneuvered her boat underneath the pilings and tied it up beneath her cabin.

Strange that her storage box was unlocked, but her keys were inside where she had left them, so she figured she had forgotten to click it shut in her preoccupation with Alex's account. Besides, the lock was a keyless entry and only she knew the code—she and Alex, who she had given it to "just in case" when she first bought the place.

Thor held back from Stu as he waited for her to call him up from the docks before bounding inside when she called.

The next day she talked to the salesman who had sold her the inflatable boat, and on his recommendation ordered a smaller back-up engine, which he told her they would come out to mount the next day.

"Not everyone believes in handling it this way, Miss, but I've known plenty of folks who were mighty glad they had things set up this way to get them out of a jam."

She trusted what he said. So far, everything he had told her had been accurate.

"One more thing I'd do if I were you," he said as she began to leave. "I'd put another 5-gallon gas can in there for your shore trips. I know it's more weight and all, but it should slide right under one of the seats and I think you'll be glad you did it."

A slushy, late spring snow was falling as she drove home, but with the temperature hovering around thirty-eight degrees, it would be melted before the next afternoon. After hanging her jacket on the peg behind the door, she threw a couple of logs into the woodstove and put some water on for tea, stopping to pick the feather Joe had given to her up from the counter, and wondering how it had gotten there from the place inside the bookcase where she had last left it tucked inside an old book.

Chapter Twenty-Four
Down Time

It was just over a week later when Alex called her.

"We're over in Kodiak," he said, "and should be heading back to Juneau next week."

Alex sounded good, especially when he talked about Emily and how well she had taken to the sea. He mentioned that the *Driftfeather* had performed well and that the investment had proven to be a good one.

When she told him about the foreclosure notice, there was a long hesitation before he answered.

"That's just not possible, Mara. I paid a year in advance. I know you took a chance on me, but you have to believe me that I paid it."

"I know what a shock this must be to you, Alex. I also want you to know that I absolutely believe you and I want you to remember that."

She proceeded to tell him how she had paid off the overdue money and of her plans to troubleshoot the problem once he returned.

"You bet I kept every one of those receipts," he told her. "I have them with my bank records in a safe deposit box at the bank. I also made copies and have them at home in a fireproof box. And, no, I didn't make any withdrawals from that account."

She reassured him again, even asking to speak to Emily so that she could reinforce her faith in Alex and his integrity. She hoped she hadn't ruined their trip home with the worry of it all, and told herself that it was probably just a clerical error.

Just to be safe, she followed up with Lessis to make sure her funds had cleared and been deposited in the account for the *Driftfeather*, making a particular point to ask for a statement from the bank saying that any foreclosure proceedings had been stopped and that Alex was not in arrears. Cleaning up his credit records would take more time, but she was assured that with his presentation of the deposit receipts, the bank would make sure that was accomplished.

Since there was nothing more she could do, she decided to spend the next week camping out along the coast and taking samples for her study on coastal plankton. Since spring weather in Southeast could be unpredictable, she brought along two full 5-gallon cans of gas and a three-week supply of both dog food and food for herself. She planned to sleep in the raft, but brought along a tent just in case, as well as plenty of raingear. She also brought along a portable water purifier and some extra flares in addition to her regular supplies.

She hadn't seen Stu for a couple of days and when a knock on his door went unanswered, she figured he must have gone out of town. With no one trustworthy around to tell about her plans, she notified the harbormaster of where she would be and of her expected return, then she climbed through the trap door, made a particular point to ensure that the supply box that held her keys was locked, swung around to the steps to pick up Thor, and headed up the coast.

The first half of the week went by uneventfully. With long sunny days and crisp nights filled with the green and pink waves of the northern lights, she and Thor explored miles of pristine shoreline and slept soundly in the gentle lap of the waves.

Twice each day she would beach the dinghy and take a long walk with Thor, bringing the shotgun along for good measure. Although it gave her a sense of security to have it, she didn't have to use it, even when a brown bear and two first year cubs came walking out of the brush as she and Thor were returning to the boat.

Since it was low tide, there was plenty of beach to put distance between them, and the sow and her young never even looked her way, although she was fully aware that the bears knew she was there. Because the tide was coming in, the raft floated out easily, and for that she was glad. Although the bear encounter had been a special moment for sure, she didn't really want to test the tolerance of the animals, especially when she had a dog with her.

At night she used the cement-filled bucket to anchor the dinghy away from shore. Although any animal that wanted to could have swum out to her, somehow she felt more secure this way. On the fourth night, when the rain started, she learned that the 5-gallon bucket she carried was a necessary accessory.

By the fifth night, she decided to beach the dinghy and find a way to get a good night's sleep. Somehow she managed to secure the inflatable raft on shore and rig up her tent over the top of it so that little water got in. For good measure, because she was so close to the high-tide line, she tied the bowline to a tree and also threw the anchor onto the beach.

When the storm ended three days later, she had actually managed to get some sleep and was ready to tackle refloating her raft. It was harder than she had imagined it would be, and would have been impossible if the back end weren't already partly buoyed by the large waves of an extra high incoming tide.

She had been careful with the motors, making sure that she tipped them up so their propellers wouldn't get bent or dinged. When she tested them each, one by one, she was relieved to find they started up without any problem.

Her shoulders ached from the strain and her left one had a searing knife-like pain boring into the backside of the joint. It seemed serious, but she could still use the arm and so she focused on getting home, making it just hours before the harbormaster had planned to launch a search. She had, he informed her, been three days overdue.

Chapter Twenty-Five
Java Java

By the end of another week, Stu's cabin remained empty. Although it was unlike him to be gone for this long, could it be that he was on vacation and had just chosen not to tell her—especially in view of his recent cranky demeanor?

Mara pondered the situation, but only for a moment. Right now she was busy trying to figure out her own life's direction, and Stu really didn't enter into the equation except that he had been a rather constant presence in her life since she had moved to Juneau.

After the difficulties of her last trip, the idea of boating up the coastline had lost some of its appeal, at least for now. So Biological had stalled, too, since her contacts at OR&P had lost some of their grant money.

Since she had paid up Alex's money due on the *Driftfeather*, things seemed to have stabilized in that arena, too, as evidenced by recent bank statements showing no unusual activity. Being that things had settled down on all fronts, and in an impulsive move that marked her new persona as a businesswoman, she purchased a small wood-frame building near the deep-water docks, and set up a new business venture called KonaJane's.

For now she planned to purchase her roasted coffee directly from a small business in Kealekakua, Hawaii that had impressed her with the quality of its beans. If things panned out, though, she was willing to consider their proposal to set up a coffee-roasting operation in her new business—an idea that intrigued her and seemed like a natural way to expand when the time was right.

Alex had been delayed another month, mostly because he had decided to follow Doug and the *Storm Roamer* into Homer, where the two planned to make some modifications on both seiners' sleeping quarters. It was all based on the fact that Emily needed some privacy from the rest of the crew, and Doug's agreement that it made sense to outfit both seiners the same way in keeping with their past history as sister vessels.

Doug had also assured Alex that he had the contacts to get the job done right, and so the two formed a friendly business alliance of sorts—and why not? From Mara's perspective, Doug had a lot to offer from his long experience as a fisherman, and she could think of no one better, really, to mentor Alex than he.

Since the night of Alex and Emily's wedding, she had softened her position on her ex-husband, even leaning toward complete forgiveness of any wrongs—perceived or real—that had come between them. Who wouldn't have been driven to near madness or hysteria by the events of both their recent pasts?

Maybe, on some level, she had contributed to the demise of their marriage without even realizing it. Whatever the case, she had done her best and she was now convinced that he had, too. At least the resentment was gone now, and that was its own tremendous relief. The future was wide open and there was nowhere to go but up from the emotional hole into which they both had fallen because of circumstances completely beyond their control.

By the time Alex returned late in May, KonaJane's was ready for the first cruise ship to arrive.

"I'd like ta be yer first customer before ya get busy with the *touri,*" Sal's familiar voice called across the currently empty shop.

"Sal?" Mara exclaimed. "Sal!"

Rushing across the room, she hugged the woman who had so often shown up just when she needed someone to lean on. Hanging a *closed* sign on the door, she pulled the shades, whipped up two fresh-brewed cups of Kona, and sat down with her friend to catch up on the latest news about her life. Thor, as usual, lay near her feet with his chin on his paws.

"Joe's fine," Sal said in response to her question. "Matter 'a fact, he'll be joinin' me here tomorrow, soon as he finishes up seein' ta Della back in Glenallen."

"What's up with Della?"

"Finally got that surgery on her arm," Sal answered. "Got it done at that famous clinic in Minnesota, but had to stay a coupla weeks at a recovery center back there before she could come home."

Sal took a sip of her coffee. "Yup, they treated her right at St. Otto's. Gotta think of some way to say thanks for the great care."

"Will her arm be okay?"

"Jest about good as new—at least that's what they're sayin'," Sal answered. "Jest about good as new."

"So, what brings you to Juneau, another honeymoon for you and Joe?" Mara laughed.

"Wish that was the case," Sal said, taking another sip of her Kona. "Good coffee, Jane."

Mara smiled and shifted her foot, which had gone to sleep with Thor resting up against it.

"Nope. Ain't gonna be no honeymoonin' this trip," Sal said. "Gotta clean up Joe's brother's estate."

"Oh . . . gosh, I'm sorry . . . I know Joe said he had a brother."

"Yeah, you know what they say, ya can pick yer friends, but not yer . . ."

Sal stopped talking for a moment as the two sat in a comfortable silence.

"I guess in the end it all turned out okay," she said. "At least Stu owed up to his fatherly responsibility and paid fer Della's surgery, though it don't no way make up for his abandonin' her when she was young."

"Stu?" Mara said, focusing on the somewhat unusual name.

"Yup. Stuart James Michael—Joe's youngest brother and Della's father. I guess he lived somewhere along the harbor. Died a lung cancer last week. Wasn't sick long, either. Just kinda up and died at the hospital back in Minnesota after visitin' Della.

We got the call the mornin' after it happened. Guess Della had put Joe and mine's name on her papers as people to be notified if anything happened to her."

Mara tried to quell the adrenaline that was racing through her veins at the unbelievable news Sal had just dropped on her. Of course, there was no certainty that it was her next-door neighbor, Stu, who was Joe's brother, but then, Stu had seemed familiar to her right from the start—and liked to talk using limericks, like Joe.

"What the hell's wrong with ya, Jane? Ya feelin' okay? Ya look like ya jest seen a ghost."

Chapter Twenty-Six
It's Only Right . . .

Once Mara had recovered from the shock of learning, not only of Stu's death, but also of his relationship to both Joe and Della, she met up with Sal again at KonaJane's to talk about Stu's memorial.

"Stu lived next door to me," she said, laughing when Sal was the one who looked surprised this time.

"Well, ain't much point ta holdin' a memorial as far as I can see," Sal said in her usual direct manner. "He's already fried and Joe gave his ashes to Della, though heaven knows why the hell she'd want 'em—but I guess bein' as Stu's her father and bein' as he paid for her surgery, I shouldn't be the one ta condemn Della's forgivin' heart. And ya say he was yer next-door neighbor? That's jest plain weird, Jane. I mean, scary weird, ya know?"

"I'm not sure how long he's been in Juneau or who he knows, really," Mara said. "I've only known him a few months, and I can't recall seeing anyone ever visit . . ."

She stood to clear the empty coffee cups from the table, waiting to see what Sal would say.

When Sal said nothing, she said, "You know, Sal, even though Stu got kinda crotchety near the end—and could be as gruff as any old sourdough I've ever met—well, he seemed like a half-decent guy underneath it all, even in spite of himself."

"Well, half-decent is a step up from what Joe thinks a him," Sal said.

"I don't know if you know I'm half owner of a seiner now . . . ," Mara said.

Sal stood, took the cups from Mara's hands, and carried them to the sink behind the front counter.

"Good heavens almighty, Jane, course I know 'bout the seiner."

Sal was eerie sometimes. Mara didn't even ask her how she knew. She had had this kind of encounter with the old woman too many times to even question what she said. The only thing she knew with certainty was that Sal was solidly in her corner and so was Joe.

"Well, I was starting to say that Stu went out on the *Driftfeather* with my business partner, Alex and . . ."

"Ah, the *Driftfeather*," Sal said in a tone that almost sounded reminiscing. "Such a fine seiner. Sound, too. They don't build 'em any better . . ."

Suddenly Sal stopped reminiscing. "So, you was sayin' somethin' about takin' Stu out on the seiner?"

"I'm just wondering if maybe we should have some kind of small memorial, Sal? Invite some of the neighbors and folks around town, you know. No one should die without anyone noticing, it's just not right."

"I'll talk to Joe 'bout it when he calls me tonight," Sal said.

"We could have it at my place or even at Stu's cabin," Mara said.

"Well, it'd be easy enough bein' as yer right next door. Ya sure ya want all them folks traipsin' through yer place?"

"Maybe not, but we could have it at the park across the street, or even at the bar he used to visit right down from where he lived."

"I like the bar idea. That way, those of us that want some anesthetic to git us through the dang memory fest can, and the rest can say whatever it is they want 'bout Stu's sorry good-fer-nothin' soul—Lord forgive me," Sal sputtered.

"You talk to Joe and let me know and I'll take care of the rest," Mara said. "Now that I own a business, it should be easy to get support from another business owner—at least I hope it works that way."

"Fair 'nuff, Jane."

Walking over to Mara, Sal suddenly put her hands on her shoulders and pulled her downward while reaching up to kiss her on the cheek.

"Yer a good woman, Jane, jest like Joe always said ya was and jest like he said yer pa was."

A knock on the door broke up their conversation as Mara lifted the shade, turned the *closed* sign to *open*, and let in a couple of customers who were trying to come in out of the rain.

"Yes, a good cup of Kona would take the chill off, and I have some homemade chocolate chip cookies and . . ."

When she looked up, Sal was just outside the door, walking toward the center of town.

Chapter Twenty-Seven
Stu's Memorial

Stu's memorial ended up being held two weeks later just as planned, with a larger-than-expected crowd gathered at the bar for the Saturday afternoon event. Mara listened as more than one old codger raised a glass to the old fisherman, many citing instances where Stu had lent them a hand while out at sea, and with most mentioning that they wondered where he had gone after retiring several years ago.

"If it hadn't been for ole Stu towin' me away from shore, I woulda lost my seiner and the biggest catch o' the year after that storm," one old guy, who called himself Dickie, said.

"Well, sure as ole Stu could drink any man under the table, he could sober up faster'n an eagle snatchin' a fish if ya needed help," another said.

"Never knew he was even sick. Thought he moved north or somethin'," a third person said.

All in all, it looked like Stu had left a better footprint on the earth than she—or even his own brother, Joe—had given him credit for, even though she could hardly contain her disgust at the rambling, phony tribute that Lessis gave.

"Many of you here know me from my role as your police officer," Lessis began, "and I believe most of you would agree that I was fair . . ."

Mara slid away from the ceremony, ducking into the restroom to escape Lessis's self-tribute. Maybe, if she were lucky, he would be done when she returned, but unfortunately, he was just getting around to talking about Stu when she got back.

"Stu and I were friends. I think most everyone here knew that. Why, there wasn't a thing I wouldn't do for the old man if he asked me, although I mostly kept those good deeds to myself."

Mara rolled her eyes and shifted uncomfortably in her chair.

"It stands to reason that that was the very reason he came to me for help when the cancer first started to rear its ugly head. Though I don't wanna brag, it was me that got Stu lined up for his trip south, me that set up the trust for his dear daughter, Della—hello Della, darlin' sure happy you could make it here today—and me who kept word about all the goin's-on quiet so ole Stu could retain the privacy he valued so much."

As Lessis continued rambling on about his pivotal role in Stu's life, Della dabbed at her eyes with a tissue, while Sal brought more than one beer back to the table for herself and Joe. By the time it was Joe's turn to speak, darkness had descended on Juneau and people were beginning to filter out of the bar.

"I just want to tell you all thanks for comin' here today and thanks for honorin' Stu," Joe said, when it was his turn to talk.

Pausing for several seconds as if to think, Joe finished by saying, "I guess that's it. That's all I got to say." Then he sat down, took a long swig of his beer, stood again, helped Della then Sal up from their chairs, gave Mara a nod, and shuffled out of the bar.

Before they left, Mara managed to stop them for a moment, asking Della if she would be in town for long. Since Joe and Sal would be taking Della back to Glenallen in the morning, there wouldn't be time for a real visit, but she at least had time to learn that the surgery on Della's arm was expected to result in a complete return of function, something Della assured her would never have happened without the help of her wonderful father, Stu.

Luckily, Della couldn't see the look on Joe's face—a look Mara recognized as something between disgust and resignation. Joe had already filled her in on some of the details of his estrangement from Stu—about how Stu had abandoned Della at birth, and now had apparently bought her love even though it had been he who had looked out for her all these years.

She hugged Sal, then put her arms around Joe and hugged him, too, holding the old man long enough to infuse his spirit with all the love she could muster.

"Thank you for coming and for bringing Della," she told Joe. "I know how hard it was for you to do and I wouldn't have expected any less."

When Joe looked up, his eyes looked tired, revealing an unusual vulnerability to his normally stoic spirit.

"We'll be seein' ya soon enough, Jane," Sal said. "Gotta come back down ta clean out Stu's cabin and probly put it up fer sale since Della's still recoverin' and says she wants to stay near her mother in Glenallen."

The sight of Alex and Emily coming through the door pulled Mara away from any more talk with Sal, as she went over to tell them how glad she was they had gotten here, even though they had just missed Stu's memorial.

"Tried our best to make it," Alex said, "but got slowed down by a storm outside of Cordova and had to hole up for a day."

And so was the day of Stu's memorial after which Mara stayed to help the bar owner clean up, handily avoiding Lessis's attempts to corner her alone in the process.

Chapter Twenty-Eight
Past Revelations

Thor was not in is usual spot at the foot of her bed when Mara woke up the next morning. Instead, she found him lying near the front door, upon which he kept pushing gently with his nose. Thinking he needed to go out, she threw on some clothes and prepared to go out early for their morning walk around the harbor.

"Della?" she said, as Thor put his paws up on the shoulders of the slightly built Native woman who was standing in front of her cabin when she opened the door.

"Uncle Joe and Sal are next door looking for some of my pa's papers," Della said. "I wanted to see you before we left. Not much chance yesterday at the memorial. It was nice—what you did for my pa."

"Walk with me?" Mara said, "or do you want to come in for coffee?"

"We can walk," Della answered.

"I see he's still got the wolf medallion," Della said, fingering the hand-beaded moose- hide medal that her mother, Mary, had made for Thor.

"And I still have the quill bracelet your mother made for me," Mara said, showing Della her wrist.

Impulsively, she reached out and hugged the young woman into whose life she had been thrust when she found her bleeding from a gunshot wound in front of the motel where Della had been the night manager.

"My mother married Henry," Della said, referring to the security guard at the motel.

"He seems like a good man," Mara said.

"He is," Della answered.

Della, in every encounter they'd, had been a woman of few words, but she was also one of those rare people who, when they spoke in short sentences, said volumes.

"My mother is happy now."

"Then I'm happy for both her and for you."

"She was worried about my arm. Henry was, too. Now it's fixed."

"That's such wonderful news, Della."

The two women watched as Thor took off after a couple of eagles. It was all in good fun. The eagles regularly liked to sit on pilings along the docks and flushing them was sport for Thor, who liked to watch them fly up and then sit right back down where they had been.

"Uncle Joe, Mary, Henry, none of them could afford it," Della said.

"You mean the surgery?"

"Yes, the surgery," Della replied.

"It's only because of my father I could have it done. He sent me the money when he heard."

Mara knew that Stu had lived frugally and had no idea what his net worth had been, but if he had seen fit to finally care for the daughter he had abandoned at birth, then perhaps he had come through for Della after all. Better late than never.

"Uncle Joe won't get over it," Della said, as she continued to reveal bits and pieces of her life.

"You mean his anger at your father for abandoning you?"

"That and the war and the fire," Della answered.

"C'mere, Thor," Mara called, snapping a leash to his collar when he returned. "You can't be running off like that. You're gonna get me in trouble."

As much as she hated to restrict Thor, listening to Della on this rare occasion when she wanted to talk meant that she couldn't allow running after him to distract her right now.

"What about the war, Della?"

"Mary didn't tell me about this until lately," Della began. "Uncle Joe fixed my father up with my mother, then when she got pregnant and I was born, he put his name on the papers and then took off. No one could find him for a long time. I heard Uncle Joe call him a draft dodger. Said he went to Canada. Uncle Joe also said that when my father came back, they didn't arrest him 'cause of me."

"I heard there was a lot of that during the Vietnam War," Mara said, "Men marrying women and getting them pregnant so the government would let them out of the draft."

"Then, when my father did come back, he stayed with Uncle Joe and his family for a while."

"I didn't know that," Mara said.

"One day Uncle Joe had to go into Anchorage to the VA. He had to be gone about four days. It was winter and my Aunt Betty sent my father out to get some wood—told him to clean out the woodstove first. My father told her that was Joe's job, but I guess he did it anyway."

Mara could almost picture Stu spouting off at Joe's wife the way she had seen him do to others, and even to herself.

"During the night, the cabin caught fire. My mother said my father put the ashes from the stove in a pile in the snow outside the house instead of spreading them around like you're supposed to, and when the wind came up that night it kindled the ashes and blew them toward the house. They caught the porch on fire and then the house. Everyone was sleeping. By the time they woke up, it was too late."

"So that explains the house fire," Mara said simply.

"All my cousins and my Aunt Betty were gone," Della said. "I remember my mother crying for weeks. She said that my father just didn't take the time to do it right because he didn't want to tend to the stove. All the time she kept talking about losing her only sister—talking about why she didn't feel the flames herself bein' as they were identical twins, and how she could have run to save Betty if she had been a good sister."

"But how could she have known?" Mara asked.

"My mother and Betty always knew. Everyone always talked about that. But my mother was sick that night and the doctor had given her some medicine that made her sleep, and so she didn't know. She said it was the first time she didn't know."

"It must have been horrible for your mother."

"For a long time, she wouldn't talk to no one about it," Della said.

"And where was your father that night, Della?"

"He was at the bar. When Uncle Joe got home the next day, my father begged his forgiveness, but Uncle Joe wouldn't listen. The day after the funerals, both my father and Uncle Joe left Hoonah and no one knew where they went. Some say Uncle Joe went lookin' for my father with an ax. I don't know if that's true."

Mara cringed at the thought, imagining the pain Joe must have endured at learning that not only was his whole family gone, but gone because of the actions of his own brother, be they intentional or not.

"Over the years I heard stories," Della said. "Sometimes I heard that my father was a fisherman out in the Gulf. He never came back. My mother never said anything bad about him, but she never said anything good either. She just told me he was gone and it was just me and her.

"Once in a while, Uncle Joe would send money. There were stories that he lived on the ferries. Some people said he was a shaman. After my gunshot, he came around and brought Sal with him. They helped my mother care for me, but they only came sometimes.

"One day I got a check in the mail, along with a letter. My father said he had heard about what happened and that he was dying and he wanted to make things right. He said he knew the money couldn't make up for the past, but maybe it could make for a better future."

The two walked slowly back toward Mara's cabin as Della talked, this time letting Thor bound ahead.

"He visited me in the hospital, and he said he was sorry and he said he hoped he didn't burn in hell for what he had done. Then he died a few days later. My mother found out about it 'cause he left his name on my records at the hospital."

At a complete loss for words, Mara let Thor into the cabin just as Joe and Sal were coming out of Stu's place.

"Wondered where the hangin' blazes ya two went off ta," Sal bellered.

"I'm sorry, Sal," Della told her.

"Ah, I ain't mad, Della. Just couldn't figure out where ya went."

"I hope you have a safe trip," Mara said to all three, before hugging Della and whispering in her ear, "Thanks for telling me, Della."

"We'll see ya in a few," Sal called as the three took off in Joe's dualie.

"Bye," Mara called softly as she waved and watched them round the corner to the street leading down to the ferry terminal. "C'mon, Thor, I think I need another walk."

Chapter Twenty-Nine
Are You Kidding Me?

By the middle of May, Joe and Sal had just about finished cleaning out Stu's cabin and were in the process of resealing and rechinking the logs where needed inside.

KonaJane's was doing well now that the cruise ships were starting to come in—enough so that Mara had hired three college students to handle things through the summer, freeing her up to follow up on a couple of small jobs sent to So Biological from the Homer office of Ocean Research and Preserve.

As usual, she climbed down through the trap door to her inflatable boat on one unusually balmy late morning, before swinging around to the floating dock to pick up Thor.

"Found this in Stu's papers," Sal called down, as Mara was idling in her boat at the foot of the stairs waiting for Thor to jump in.

"What is it?" she called up, surprised when Sal read her the code to the lock box where she kept her boat supplies on the pilings under her cabin.

"It says, *Mara's lockbox* in Stu's handwriting next to it. Figure you must have gave it to Stu to watch out fer yer place when ya was out."

"Thanks, Sal. I'll change the combination when I get back."

The fact was, she had already changed the combination after finding the box unlocked back after her first long trip out on the raft—the same trip from which she had returned to find Stu with his hand on her front door. Well, it was a moot point now that Stu was dead, anyway, so she put it out of her mind and set out for the north shore, which had become her favorite research location.

The weather that day was unusually warm and sunny, making it easy to linger after collecting the samples she needed for OR&P. As usual, she took

Thor ashore, but this time she carried her shotgun since bears were up from hibernation and roaming around in the area with their young cubs.

She had taught Thor to stay quiet around animals, a trait that was very important in an Alaskan dog since dogs resembled wolves, a natural predator to many species. The fact that Thor was also part wolf made it even more important that she retain control over him in the wild.

What had emerged from this partnership was a beautiful relationship, where Thor was able to read subtle cues in her body language and was also able to communicate with her in the same way. Occasionally, she would have to warn him to stay still, but always with just a sound or a softly spoken one-word command.

Thor had learned the hard way about porcupines when he was a pup, having come home with a snout full of quills one summer's day according to Doug. Still, she kept a close eye on him when he wandered off to sniff the scents that were so plentiful everywhere they walked, and fortunately, on this trip at least, all they came across was a fox scurrying down a trail of sedges left flattened by a bear.

When she got back into the harbor in the early evening, she noticed that the *Driftfeather* had been moved to the docks closest to her row of cabins and that the *Storm Roamer* was tied up right alongside.

There didn't seem to be any activity aboard either vessel, even though she slowed to putt around both seiners and even called up for Alex or Emily to answer. When she pulled up to the floating stairs, Sal was standing there watching.

"She's as fine today as the day me and Bert first bought 'er," Sal said, her voice taking on an unusually wistful tone.

"She?" Mara asked. "Are you talking about one of the seiners?"

"The *Driftfeather*," Sal answered. "I sold it after Bert died. Couldn't afford to keep up with it. Kinda lost my passion fer the sea 'bout then, too. Ya either come back from losin' one ya love ta the sea, or ya don't. That's when I sold 'er."

Once again, Mara was at a loss for words. In the span of the very few months she had lived in Juneau, she had discovered one truth after another and after another about those whose lives had touched hers. The irony of it all didn't escape her. Her entire time in Alaska had been that way. Maybe that's what the saying she saw carved on a paper mache moose she had bought at an art shop in Wasilla meant:

If you think life is a search, Alaska is where you'll find yourself!

Boy, would she like to meet the author of those words. They sure had proven to be true for her so far!

"Why'd you git so quiet, Jane? Didja think I didn't know ya bought my old seiner? I jest didn't wanna tell ya yet—ruin yer experience or creep ya out or anythin'."

"I don't even know what to say, Sal," Mara answered. "I mean, what could I even say?"

"Well, ya could start by sayin' yer glad it's my boat and not some piece a trash from someone who don't know nothin' about seiners."

Mara just looked at the old woman before putting the raft in reverse and backing around to the place she kept it under her cabin.

"I'll unlock the cabin door if you want to come in," she told Sal.

"No can do this time, Jane. Though there's more I need ta tell ya startin' with the fact that that other seiner over there—the *Storm Roamer*—used ta be mine an' Bert's, too."

She stopped the dinghy right there in the water and just stared at Sal.

"Buck up, Jane. Me 'n Joe need ta head home at first light, but be assured that ya done good in choosin' my ole seiner fer yer own and, if'n love travels the way I think it does—ya know, in mysterious ways—so did yer ex ole man in buyin' the *Storm Roamer*."

"Godspeed to you and Joe tomorrow," Mara said simply. For right now, she had heard all the information she could handle.

Chapter Thirty
Casual Invitation?

Mara's week didn't take an upturn when she went into KonaJane's after dropping her samples in the mail to OR&P the next day. She had chosen to walk to work, bringing Thor along as much for company as to let him have a day out of the house.

She was surprised when Doug Williams walked in around eleven, and even more surprised when he said he wondered if she had time to sit for a cup of coffee. Instead of staying inside, the two sat at one of the three tables out front, where they could enjoy views of both the harbor and the downtown area.

Doug told her he was in town to resupply for a job he was going out on later in the week, and told her that Alex was considering following in the *Driftfeather* just to get more experience. Alex had indeed mentioned that he might be going out again soon, so the news was not a total surprise, but the fact that the two men had formed such a congenial relationship put her a bit off center.

"You know, I think it'd be fun if you came along, Mara. And I'm not trying to be funny here or anything. I'd also like to get Thor used to the seiner again. It's getting to be time for me to spend some quality time with him before he forgets who I am."

"But he's doing so well here," she said. "Do you really want to take him out to sea where he can't run and play?"

"Just for about three weeks. At least, that's the plan."

"Well, now that Alex has Emily, I'm not sure they would appreciate having me along," she said, knowing full well that both Alex and Emily had been begging her to come out with them for weeks.

"There's plenty of room on the *Storm Roamer.* I even spruced up the cabin area so it would be like the one Alex fixed up for Emily on the *Driftfeather.*"

"I don't know if it would be a good idea, Doug. I mean, I'm glad we're on good terms after everything that happened and all that, but I'm just not willing to pretend that what we had together didn't end badly."

Doug was smart enough not to pressure her, although the seriousness of his tone told her that he meant the offer he had extended.

"It's something I'm not proud of," he told her, "and what happened to our marriage—it's something I wish had never happened, but it is what it is and I can't undo it. Think about what I said. We're not set to leave till Saturday and that's two and a half days away."

"I'll talk to Alex," she told him, gently pushing Thor's nose off her foot as he nuzzled it beneath the table.

"You can find me on my seiner," Doug said, carrying the now empty cups inside before leaving.

Chapter Thirty-One
Seeing the Light

Things were getting just plain weird lately, even to the point that Mara was seriously considering joining Doug on the *Storm Roamer*. When she thought about it, it made sense as she would be able to help Thor adjust to life back at sea, and she would also be able to observe Alex's handling of the *Driftfeather*. Still, hadn't she just months earlier abandoned all her friends and even dumped a perfectly good SUV in the Knik River?

As out of character as Doug's behavior just prior to the divorce had been, so too had her reaction been less than mature. The more she started thinking about it, the more she began to realize that circumstances beyond what most couples ever face had driven them both to behave erratically.

On the other hand, what were the chances that they wouldn't repeat the same mistakes the next time a crisis came about? Whatever the case, she was now in her late thirties and Doug was forty. Maybe it was time to stop all the emotional hysteria and treat him like the good person he had always been. It was only a fishing trip and the two of them had always worked well together.

"When can I start bringing my things aboard?" she called up to Doug from her dinghy.

The smile that flashed across his face seemed to erase everything bad that had ever come between them.

"Anytime you're ready."

"I have to write Sarah first, then I'll be back."

Dear Sarah, I'm sorry. Tell everyone for me, okay. I'm fine. I ran into Doug here in Juneau. More later. Love, Mara

The fact of the matter was that she knew Sarah would welcome the letter, and that she wouldn't harbor any resentment for the way she had behaved. In all the years they had been friends, and through all the two of them had been through—through separations, challenges, anger, and hurt—she and Sarah were friends.

The distance she had put between them had been necessary. How else could she have examined the traumas of the past two years—figured out who she was—without breaking out on her own?

Whatever had prompted this change of heart mystified her as much as she was sure it would everyone else in her life, yet somehow it all felt natural and right. She didn't need a psychiatrist to tell her to listen to her heart and soul, although she could appreciate why some might think it wise to see one. Maybe her new start had turned out to be more than just cutting loose from the past and relocating.

It was like a lightbulb on life suddenly went off inside her brain. *The new start, Mara, began with you! Not with physically changing your world, but with changing how you looked at your place within it.*

She wasn't at all sure what being cooped up on a seiner with her ex-husband was going to bring in the way of adventure, but one thing she knew, and that was that she was open to finding out. And it wouldn't be about recapturing the past, or exploring what went wrong, or agonizing over past feelings, it would be about embracing the future without baggage or restriction.

"C'mon, Thor. Let's go fishing."

As she walked through the cabin to the front door, the feather Joe had given her suddenly drifted to the floor from its place high up on a bookshelf. Stopping in her tracks, she watched it whirl mysteriously in the air currents of the house before landing near the table where she often sat. Had she actually seen the two red dots flicker for a moment in the process, or had the sunlight that had begun pouring through the window into the room simply been playing tricks on her eyes?

When she stooped to pick it up, it slipped from her fingers, again whirling to the floor before she was able to catch it and put it back on the shelf.

Chapter Thirty-Two
The Magic of Spring

Right after leaving the *Storm Roamer*, Thor cut his front paw on a piece of metal sticking out of the ground, which required a trip to the vet. The bottom line was that he would heal okay, but the bad news was that the vet recommended he remain on shore so that the wound could be regularly cleaned and he would have access to care if necessary.

Together, Mara and Doug decided that it would be best if they followed the vet's advice, so Mara hired one of the college students from KonaJane's who just happened to be in pre-vet at UAF. Sandy would clean Thor's wound as instructed, as well as housesit at Mara's cabin, providing less stress for Thor.

"I'm surprised you decided to still come along," Doug told Mara. "But I'm glad you did."

Why wouldn't she? It was strictly business and totally on the up and up, with Derrk Stanley and another crew member on board, and she was anxious to learn about the performance of both the *Storm Roamer* and the *Driftfeather*, as well as gather some deep-water samples for So Biological.

On board the *Driftfeather* would be Alex, Emily, and two deckhands. The two seiners would travel close to each other and would remain in regular contact.

By day three out at sea, everyone aboard both seiners was enjoying the amazing appearance of one of the most beautiful springs any of them had seen in years. By the middle of the second week, they were located about 50 miles off the southern tip of Alaska's Panhandle. For the last day, they had held fast in an area that seemed to be in the heart of the gray-whale migration and had also noticed that the humpbacks were beginning to arrive back in Alaska.

You can tell individual humpbacks by the unique markings on their tails, Mara could almost hear Stu's voice say inside her head. He had often talked about the amazing whales. She smiled as she remembered how the double blowholes on top of their barnacled heads, as well as their behavior known as fluking, had always fascinated him. Certainly there was nothing more beautiful than seeing one of the 50-foot, 75,000-pound mammals blow a 20-foot spray into the air, before arching its back to dive, and flipping its massive tail just before disappearing from sight.

"Look, that one has a calf," she told Doug, whipping her camera from her pocket to try to get a shot.

"I'll radio Alex and let them know," Derrk Stanley said. "I think there's another one with a calf up ahead."

"I'd forgotten how much I loved this," Mara said, spontaneously grabbing Doug's arm just like she had done so many times before.

"You always were happiest at sea," Doug said, placing one arm around her.

And with that simple exchange, Doug Williams and Mara Benson Edwards Williams Benson were a couple again.

Through the next several days, they would exchange thoughts on how they had drifted apart, but they would choose to dwell on none of it. This was the way it was supposed to be and this was the life they had chosen to live together before the barrage of heartache had torn them apart.

For now there was little talk of the past, and not much talk of the future. For now there was just the present and for each of them, that was all they needed—that, and to not let anything pull them apart again.

Chapter Thirty-Three
Emily

Just south of Cordova, Alex radioed that Emily had started vomiting uncontrollably.

"I've got no choice but to get her in to the nearest hospital," he radioed.

Doug had been at the radio when the call came in.

"We're probably about four hours out of Cordova, Alex. If you can position yourself behind us, maybe you can put one of your crew at the wheel while you check on Emily and let us guide you in."

"Okay," Alex replied. "I've got a guy I've been training right here with us."

"Just make sure you're keeping a close eye on him, because we're going to have to fight this storm I've been watching move in, here."

"Okay," Alex said again, straining to relax the white-knuckle grip he had on the wheel as he signaled his crewmate to take it over.

"Meanwhile, I'm going to put Mara in the back to watch you for extra measure."

"Okay, Cap," Alex replied, referring to Doug by the nickname his peers had given him long ago.

"Also, I don't want to alarm you or Emily, Alex, but I think it'd be best to put her in her survival suit. Mara's getting into hers right now and I'll be doing the same soon."

"Survival suit. Do you know something I don't?"

Wasn't putting on survival suits was always a last ditch effort right before sinking or being thrown overboard?

"Nothing you don't know, Alex, and nothing you can't handle," Doug said, sensing his alarm. "We've got a storm coming in a bit stronger than I expected, and if we get into any kind of trouble whatsoever, there isn't going to be time to help both Emily and yourself. Don't forget to get your own ready, too."

"Okay," Alex replied for the third time.

"Don't pull it all the way on her yet, but get her feet in so all she has to do is pull it over her shoulders and head if she needs it. It's not like she's going to be getting up and walking around. Have your other crewman nearby, too, to help with her if you need to. Make sure the crews got theirs, too. Now let's take these seiners in."

Doug had been right about one thing. The storm had come up fast and it had come up strong. Within the hour, both the *Driftfeather* and the *Storm Roamer* were being tossed in 15-foot seas, making it a struggle to keep moving into the waves as the wind kept pushing them sideways against the surf.

"I want your man to back off just a bit now," Doug radioed to Alex. "Mara says she can see the whites of your eyes and that's too close in these kind of seas."

For the next two hours, both seiners struggled against the storm as they moved through driving rain and gale-force winds toward the shore. As instructed, Alex and his crewman managed to keep the *Driftfeather* far enough back so as not to endanger the *Storm Roamer*, yet still close enough to maintain visual contact.

About thirty minutes out, Alex radioed that Emily had hit her head and was bleeding.

"Hold 'er steady, Alex. Emily conscious?"

"Yes," Alex replied.

"You're going to have to stay steady now, Alex. Can you put one of your men with Emily? We're only about fifteen minutes out now."

"I can see the shore," Alex radioed. "Emily's moaning. My crewman says she's fading in and out of consciousness."

"Stay focused on getting to shore, Alex. You're not going to be much help to her or to yourself by flipping the *Driftfeather* in these seas or banging up against the rocks because you didn't keep our cool. Now take the wheel back from your crewman and do exactly what I tell you to do."

"I should be with Emily," Alex called.

"Alex! Stay at the wheel. Alex! You do what I tell you, you hear! You need to stay at the wheel!"

For a few seconds there was no answer, leading Doug to call back to Mara to see if she could see anything.

"I'm not sure, Doug," she called to him. "Wait, I think I see him. I do. Alex is at the wheel and they're holding steady right behind us."

"Keep her steady, Alex," Doug said, his voice flat and steady. "You're doing fine, now. Keep her steady."

Visibility had deteriorated and the wind had increased as the two seiners made their way into the safety of the harbor. Doug had already radioed the harbormaster, who had authorized emergency docking for both vessels and who had arranged for an ambulance to take Emily to the hospital located in the small seaside community of Cordova.

By evening, he had arranged for temporary docking for both the *Driftfeather* and the *Storm Roamer*, and with the help of their crews, adequately secured the seiners. The crewmembers had elected to sleep on board, but Doug and Mara had taken a room at the hotel right next to two others they secured for Derrk, and for Alex and Emily.

As it turned out, according to Alex, Emily would have to stay the night at the hospital for observation due to the circumstances of cutting her head, even though her neurological signs were stable and the medication she had been given had eased the vomiting. The other news: Emily was pregnant.

"The doctor says she shouldn't go back home on the seiner," Alex told Doug. "Right now, he wants to watch her for a day before he'll even allow her to fly."

Doug watched Alex dial his cell phone as he relayed what the doctor had said.

"Emily wants me to call her brother," he said looking up as he dialed.

Chapter Thirty-Four
Friend in Need

Thankfully, according to the doctor, Emily's baby seemed to be okay and the nausea had only been a part of the early pregnancy that was aggravated by being at sea. The doctor had also reassured Alex that the bump on Emily's head did not appear to be serious, especially since they had kept her under observation for twenty-four hours, so he released her to fly back to Juneau.

"I totally understand that you need to be with her," Mara told Alex. "Doug and I will figure out how to get the *Driftfeather* back to Juneau, or we'll leave it here till you can come back."

Her words seemed to reassure Alex and so he agreed to leave with Emily that afternoon. She also asked Alex to check on Sandy and Thor, which he said he would do as soon as they got back and found a place to stay. That got her to thinking that maybe Alex and Emily could stay in Stu's place since Joe and Sal had pretty much emptied it out—an idea that Alex quickly embraced.

"Hell's afire, she's pregnant?" Sal bellowed into the phone when Mara called her with the latest news. "No wonder she was upchuckin' her brains out on that seiner."

Not only was Sal willing to let Alex and Emily stay in Stu's cabin, but she also said that she and Joe would leave earlier than they had intended to in order to bring down the bed they planned to put in the cabin so they could use it for a getaway spot.

"The only other thing we have to—" Mara began.

"We, Jane? Somethin' about the way ya jest said *we* tells me ta ask about jest what *we* means," Sal interrupted.

Why was it simply impossible to keep anything from Sal Kindle Michael? And, so Mara told Sal about Doug and the *Storm Roamer* and the *Driftfeather* and the whole story of the trip that had somehow righted both of their lives.

"Well, hell's afire again, Jane. We was wonderin'—me and Joe that is—when ya was both gonna come ta yer senses."

"But weren't you the one who told me to get over Doug?"

"What I said was that yer man fell by the wayside's what I said, Jane. Don't mean he stayed there, accordin' ta what yer tellin' me now. My Joe, fer one's, gonna be mighty glad ta hear that, too."

Mara laughed out loud as Sal talked. In spite of everything that had happened, her heart felt lighter than it had in a long, long time.

"Ya sound like a twitterin' schoolgirl, Jane. I kin hear it in yer voice," Sal laughed back. "Now what about them seiners?"

"That's a good question, Sal. Let me get back to Alex and Emily and then I'll call you back with more details. And, Sal . . ."

"Yeah, Jane?"

"You're the best."

"Well, ya ain't fried potatas yerself, Jane," Sal said before hanging up.

Chapter Thirty-Five
Will You . . .

Doug and Mara's reunion had softened the drama surrounding Alex, Emily, and the sudden change in everyone's plans, so they took it in stride when Derrk got called Outside for a death in his family.

According to the phone conversation Mara had with Sandy, Thor's paw had just about healed and she was taking him for his daily walks, sometimes even taking him to work with her, which she said he seemed to love. She also told her that Alex and Emily had arrived and settled into Stu's old place and that Emily's brother had flown in to stay with them and help out. She also said that Alex had told her to let her know they were fine.

"The two men have been coming and going a lot so I figure that the woman—Emily, right?—must be doing okay," Sandy said. "They said to tell you that since Sal and Joe were going to fly down to Cordova to help with the seiners, they would just use the cabin a little longer and then meet you and Doug back in Juneau."

Strange, Mara had only heard of Emily's brother for the first time in Cordova. She couldn't remember meeting him at the wedding. Well, families were like that nowadays, always drifting in and out of each other's lives. Emily's brother had probably just escaped her notice or maybe hadn't been able to attend the wedding for whatever reason.

Later, over dinner that night, she filled Doug in on all the latest.

"Sal told me that she and her first husband used to own both seiners. She said she sold them after she lost him at sea."

Doug raised his eyebrows in surprise.

"Wow! Like Sal would say, I didn't see that coming, but nothing having to do with either Sal or Joe should surprise me."

He reached across the table and laid his hand over Mara's, knowing that accidents and even death at sea were a risk that all fishermen and their families faced each time they went out on another trip.

"I can't believe you're back," he told her, making her blush.

"Me either," she laughed before fixing her eyes on his.

"I know what you're thinking," he said, "and I understand how you're wondering if this is going to . . . if it can really work out this time."

"Not really. You see, as much as I wanted to blame it all on you, all that's happened since we split up . . . all of this has made me who I am right now, and that me is someone who is telling you that we both had things to learn."

Doug furrowed his brow. He had accepted full responsibility for everything that had gone wrong between them—now Mara was saying that she had somehow been part of the problem?

"I know it sounds weird," she said, sensing his confusion, "but for reasons even I don't understand, this all happened the way it was supposed to. Before, I was so impulsive and so naïve and so one-dimensional. Now, well, the truth is that I'm not afraid to lose you anymore because I'm not afraid to be alone."

Doug watched her, his eyes locking with hers. There was something different about Mara now—something stronger. It was as though she had become a better version of the wonderful person she had always been.

"I know I don't deserve this second chance," he told her, suddenly getting up from his chair and getting down on one knee right then and there in the restaurant.

Mara felt all eyes in the room look their way as she let Doug take her hand and propose.

"This time we'll have a real wedding," he said when she answered yes.

Just then, Joe and Sal walked in, catching the two in an embrace in front of the applauding crowd of diners who had joined in the excitement of the occasion.

"We're getting married—again," Mara laughed as she hugged first Sal, then Joe.

"Well, hell's a blazin', even I didn't see that one comin'," Sal said, sounding completely surprised.

Joe was surprisingly quiet. Was that a tear he was dabbing from the corner of his eye? Mara walked over to him and hugged him in the biggest bear hug she could muster.

"Are those tears of happiness or sadness?"

"I was just thinkin' about your father," Joe said. "And about how proud of you he'd be right now."

"Well, it's not like I got it right from the get-go. It's taken me a while to find true love's path, but you know, in spite of everything—well, I know it's right. It was always right with Doug. It's just that we lost sight of who we were, and I feel in the bottom of my soul that neither of us is going to let that happen to us again."

"So the two dots worked," Joe said with a deadpan expression, referring to the feather with two dots that he had given her back in Glenallen.

"So they did," she said, kissing the old man on the cheek. "But I don't think . . . I can't imagine that they will stick unless you swear to me in front of Doug and Sal right now that you will give me away at my wedding."

This time, the tears in Joe's eyes spilled down his cheeks as Sal reached over to dry them with the corner of her sleeve.

"Well, I suppose we'd better get those seiners back to Juneau so Sal and I can get some new clothes," Joe said, pulling both Doug and Mara toward his open arms and squeezing them as if he'd never let them go.

Chapter Thirty-Six
Injustice?

"Wake up, Jane!" Sal's trembling holler rang through the hotel room door as Doug and Mara were packing the remainder of their clothes in preparation for the trip back to Juneau later that morning.

All five foot two of Sal Kindle Michael pushed through the door before Doug could even finish opening it to let her in.

"The Feds got Joe. Hell's almighty, they took my Joe ta the dang slammer."

"Hold on, Sal," Doug said, guiding the old woman to a chair. "What do you mean they took Joe to the slammer?'

"Said it's embezzlement," Sal said, struggling not to cry. "Said he siphoned money outta Stu's account inta his own ta the tune of a hundred and eighteen grand. Said they found the receipts to prove it in his glove box."

"I didn't know Stu had that kind of money, Sal," Mara said. "He was always talking to me about how he was living on a fixed income and could barely get by if something broke down around the house or some emergency came up."

"I dunno, Jane. I dunno," Sal said, getting up and pacing around the hotel room. "All I know is that my Joe ain't no embezzler and now they got him locked up like a . . . like a dang criminal."

Before Mara could say anything, Doug bolted out the door, returning two hours later with a very tired and stressed-looking Joe Michael.

"I posted bail," Doug said simply. "Now we need to get back to Juneau and get to the bottom of all this."

"I'll alert my lawyer," Mara said, while helping Joe with his coat, "and ask him to refer us to someone specializing in this type of defense."

Suddenly Joe clutched his chest with one arm and lowered himself onto the bed with the help of the other. "Call 911," he gasped through lips that were as pale as Della's had been the night she was shot.

Minutes later, paramedics were taking him out Mara's cabin door on a gurney, and wheeling him along the boardwalk to the ambulance waiting on the street.

The oxygen the medics had started had already improved Joe's color and relieved some of the pain, the rest of which was eased as soon as he was given meds in the ER to alleviate what doctors were calling spasms in his heart artery.

By late afternoon, the medevac helicopter had arrived and spirited him away to Juneau with the staff allowing Sal to ride along since Joe's vital signs had remained stable for the past two hours.

Joe Michael had already survived one near-death cardiac experience, a subsequent coronary artery bypass surgery, and a full year of cardiac rehabilitation just a few years before. No one said out loud what they were all thinking. At seventy-four years of age, would Joe be able to continue to survive this latest episode with his heart? Late that evening, after stents had been placed into two of Joe's coronary arteries, everyone heaved a sigh of relief on learning that Joe Michael was feeling much better, even though incredibly tired.

Mara, Doug, and Sal took turns visiting him in the CCU, each praying silently between visits that he would be able to withstand this latest crisis. Somehow, all of them knew that they would do all they could to get to the bottom of whatever or whoever had created the circumstances that had led to Joe's present life crisis.

"Bein' as we rented out Stu's place to Alex and Emily, I'll just stay here at the hospital with my Joe," Sal said as nighttime approached, looking as tired and frail as Mara had ever seen her.

"You'll stay with Doug and me and Thor at my cabin," Mara said decisively. "It'll be a little cozy, but it's just the way it's going to be. Alex and Emily will be right next door to help out if we need them."

"I've got to fly back to Cordova and see to the seiners anyway," Doug said. "I'll leave tonight and be back here by tomorrow night."

By 9 p.m. Doug was on his way to Cordova and Sal was back at Joe's side after deciding that the short nap she took at Mara's place was all the rest she would need.

Chapter Thirty-Seven
New Information

Mara hadn't seen Emily or Alex since she had returned. As it was, she had barely had time to pick Thor up and get Sandy out of her cabin prior to flying in with Doug and Sal. When she met up with Alex the next day, he looked like he had the weight of the world on his shoulders.

"Everything okay with Emily and the baby?" she asked.

"Yeah, they're fine," Alex answered, "but there's something going on I need to talk to you about."

"Okay," she answered, inviting him in and setting them up with a fresh cup of Kona out on her deck. "I need to talk to you, too."

The thing was that she just wasn't sure how or when she should tell Alex about what had happened to Joe.

"Well, the first thing is that Emily and I have been talking that maybe the seafaring life is not for us, you know—especially now with the baby coming?"

She leaned forward to listen. Not Alex now. What was going on with everyone in her life?

"I was thinking about how I would tell you and what we could arrange with the *Driftfeather* and all that," Alex continued. "I pretty much had it worked out that I would offer to sell out my share to you—especially since you already put quite a lot on those misplaced payments, which is another thing I want to talk to you about."

She could see that the conversation was difficult for Alex. It almost sounded like he had lost his passion for fishing and all things seiner, but he had a wife now and a child on the way, so she could understand how his focus might have shifted. Maybe everything with the bank account was getting to him. It was getting to her and she was financially established. Imagine how it felt to a young man just starting out in life.

She reached out and put one hand on his and spoke slowly, telling him how much she admired his work, and that she understood that now that Emily was pregnant his priorities might have changed. One thing seemed certain: this was not the time to tell him about Joe Michael.

Alex sat there, not saying anything for a while. He looked distracted, as if organizing his thoughts. When he finally did speak, he stared at the top of the table instead of looking her in the eye like he usually did. She had always admired the way that Alex spoke directly and with full confidence. Now, though, something was different.

"Another thing is that my father had a stroke last week . . ."

"Oh, no," Mara gasped.

Maybe that explained the change in Alex's demeanor.

"He's going to be okay," he was quick to interject. "The doctors say the residual damage should be minimal, but that's another reason that I want to take Emily and move back Outside—to be near my folks now that they're getting older."

"We'll work it out, Alex."

"But that's not all of it," he continued.

She stared at him. Was it the stress? Whatever it was, he seemed to be deep in his own thoughts. Hopefully, he couldn't see the look of confusion she was struggling so hard to hide.

"Go on . . ."

"There's something funny going on with the bank. Something more than funny, something downright scary."

It was doubtful that Alex had found out about Joe, so what could the problem be?

"You know how I told you I kept a copy of all my deposit slips and receipts?"

"Yes," she answered.

"Well, I went through them all and it was just like I said, the money had been put into my account like it should have."

Mara leaned forward with her elbows resting on the table as Alex talked.

"When we got back—Emily and me—there was a lien placed against the *Driftfeather* for not just the amount that you put in to cover what they said I didn't pay, but also for the next check I know I sent in, and . . ." he said, pausing for emphasis, "and for my original down payment on the seiner, which as you know, came to close to $54,000. That with the $90,000

I financed put my share of the seiner at—well, exactly at $143, 750. I put another forty grand into it on upgrades—the skiff, fishing gear, and so on."

Mara was puzzled.

"I wonder why I didn't get a copy of that notice?"

"Me, too," Alex replied.

"So the lien is for around $180,000?" she asked, barely able to contain the adrenaline that was surging inside her.

"About that—plus or minus a few dollars," Alex answered.

He took a sip of coffee and then got up and paced around her deck before sitting back down, putting his face into his hands, and then looking right at her as he said, "Mara, you need to trust that I put all the money in there just like I said."

Just then his phone rang and he excused himself before stepping inside to talk. She was surprised that he even carried the cell phone, much less answered it while he was visiting. She had never known him to be a gadget-loving person. She watched him talk, his body language telling her that the call was urgent.

While he was talking, she walked to the railing and watched a couple of otters float by. What the heck was going on? Alex was not a liar nor had he ever given any indication that he was a thief. She had deposited some of her own money to cover the alleged loss—money that Alex now wanted to subtract from the $143,000-plus that was his share of the boat's purchase as part of the deal on selling the *Driftfeather* back to her, so the buyback he was proposing seemed fair and well thought out. The whole situation with the lien that had been placed on the *Driftfeather* had come as a shock to her, though, so how was it that Alex had had time to think this all through already? She grabbed another cup of coffee when she saw him coming back out, but before she could sit back down, he said, "I've got to go."

He was out the door before she could prompt him for an explanation. She heard the door to his cabin bang shut and heard him speaking loudly to both Emily and her brother, but she couldn't make out what he was saying.

Suddenly, she heard footsteps rushing down the boardwalk. Thor growled as the footsteps slowed and then stopped in front of her cabin. She started to go for her gun, but it was in the drawer in her bedroom and she wanted to lock her door first.

"Stay inside, Mara," she heard Alex call, but not before her door flew open and someone grabbed her and spun her around, holding a gun to her head.

"Lessis!"

"Let her go," Alex said, bursting through the door right behind him with his own gun drawn.

"Not on your life, Winron, you slimy punk," Lessis growled.

Jerking Mara's arm more tightly against her back, Lessis hissed, "Gimme the keys to your skiff."

"It's right down there—through the trap door," she said, trying to look behind her. "You don't need keys to start . . ."

Thor growled again.

"Call the mutt off or I'll put a bullet between his eyes. Now!"

"Thor! Sit! Lie down!" Mara screamed, surprised when Thor minded on the first call.

"Let her go, Lessis," Alex called.

"Put your gun down and back slowly out of here," Lessis demanded. "Do it before I lose my patience if you're as smart as you think you are."

Alex lowered his gun and backed off.

"Now shut the door behind you," Lessis barked, watching as Alex closed the door.

Mara was trembling.

"Get down in the skiff," Lessis commanded, but just as she started down the ladder, her foot slipped causing her to fall into the water where she landed beside one of the pilings, uninjured.

Gulping for air, she slid under the water, hoping that Lessis couldn't see her, and waited until she thought her lungs would explode, coming up just as Lessis roared away in her skiff. Just then, she saw Alex and another man roar off in his skiff and saw one of them raise a gun and fire.

"Thor!" She screamed. "Thor!"

Thor was there within seconds, blood dripping from his neck. Mara grabbed him and he backed up, helping pull her from the water. By now she was sobbing and others in the complex were rushing to her aid.

"Your dog went right through the window," someone said, "but it looks like the cut is superficial. Are you all right?"

"I need to call my husband," she told him.

"Let's get you inside first," someone else said.

By the time the police left a few hours later, she had managed to get ahold of Doug, who said he would be on the first flight home.

"I don't know what's going on, Mara, but you need to take Thor and get to someplace safe. I'm not going to be able to get there before this time tomorrow, if even then. A system moved in this morning and all flights are grounded."

Mara grabbed some clothes and stuffed them into a bag. She decided that she would risk taking a quick shower as much to warm up as to try to wash off the stench of what had just happened. Just as she was finishing dressing, she heard the sound of a skiff, feeling her muscles tense and her adrenaline surge as she tried to decide which exit to use. Grabbing her phone, she dialed 911.

Assured that police were on their way, she went out her front door, only to meet up with Alex and another guy. Each of them had a firm grip on Lessis's arms, which were tied securely behind his back.

"You'll be okay in your cabin now," Alex called as he handed Lessis over to the police, who had just arrived. "I'll board that window up for you later."

Chapter Thirty-Eight
Is It Over Yet?

"Lessis is in jail," Alex told her when he came back to board up her window.

He certainly looked calm for someone who had just chased a man down amidst gunfire.

"Thanks, Alex, and thanks for risking your life to chase him down. Are you okay?"

"I'm fine. I had every reason to want to go after him even before he pulled the stunt he did today," Alex said. "When I went to the bank this morning, all the money that I deposited and the money that you told me you deposited had been withdrawn from my account. When I asked Lessis for an explanation, he acted like he didn't hear me and walked away."

Mara was more livid than she believed was possible. $180,000 was exactly the amount that the Feds had accused Joe Michael of embezzling and she knew without a doubt that Joe Michael hadn't embezzled anything!

"First of all, Alex, I want you to know that I believe you," she said. "Secondly, I want you to know that we *will* get to the bottom of this, and lastly, I need to tell you that there is more to this story than I can make sense of right now, because I'm still trying to piece it all together myself, but I need you to know that it was not me who withdrew any money from that account."

"I know that, Mara. That's why I told Lessis I was going to notify the FBI of what had happened."

"What did he say?"

"I never gave him a chance to say anything," Alex said. "I just walked out and decided to deal with him later. I guess he showed us what he had to say this afternoon. In retrospect, I should have just called in the feds and let them handle confronting him."

"Well, anyone would have done the same thing," she said. "We're talking thousands—hundreds of thousands here, but even so, his reaction seems extreme."

She went on to tell Alex about Joe, his arrest, and the events that had followed—including that she had reunited with her ex-husband, Doug Williams, surprised when Alex did not seem to react with more than a slight nod of his head to the news.

"Doug's socked in over in Cordova right now, but he'll be here as soon as the weather lifts and he can get a flight out."

"I think you'll be okay now," Alex told her. "The police told me they're going to keep a man outside our cabins for the next few days, just in case anyone else at the bank feels like following Lessis's lead. They don't think anything will happen, though."

"Thank you, Alex. That helps. Does Emily know about any of this? I mean, the missing money. I know she has to know about today."

"I don't want to focus on Emily and what she may or may not know right now," he said, before quickly adding, "The baby, you know? But just so you know, she was in town for a checkup when all this with Lessis happened today. She just got back."

"Then let's keep it between us for now. Matter of fact, I could use some extra help down at KonaJane's, so maybe she would consider taking on a part-time job for a few weeks. You can tell her that you need that much time to make arrangements for the move south. That will keep her focused on something while we figure this out, okay? I'll just tell her that we had a break-in, but that the police caught the suspect."

"Sure. Okay. Good idea," Alex said so softly that she almost couldn't hear him. "I hope this stays out of the news—at least for now."

She was right to worry. Not only was something fishy going on at the bank, but there had also been a big change in Alex's demeanor—a change that she was struggling to pinpoint. His comment about the news was perplexing, too. Why would he care?

Flashing her his familiar boyish grin, Alex suddenly sprang from his chair and gave her a quick peck on the cheek.

"I'm glad you're all right," he said as she sat there dumbfounded at the way he had so abruptly reverted to his old self. "I wouldn't want to have to explain to Doug that you were nearly abducted by a deranged psycho-banker, slash, ex-cop. Now I guess I'd better get back and straighten myself out before Emily thinks there's something wrong."

"Give her my best, Alex. And thanks for capturing Lessis. I'll bet the police give you a citation for that."

"I guess they might," was all he said.

Mara needed to think. With Doug gone and stuck in Cordova for who knows how long, and with Sal staying at the hospital with Joe, she decided to take her skiff for a putt around the bay as much to get away as to check for any damage done by Lessis. Before leaving, she packed a sandwich for herself and some food for Thor.

Maybe she'd come back late tonight or maybe she'd come in early tomorrow morning. She needed however long it took to think this through, so she took enough gear and some extra food just in case, and left a note for Doug and Sal by the door. Also, on impulse, she grabbed the feather given to her months ago by Joe Michael and stuffed it into her bag.

As she was pulling away from the dock, she saw Alex wheeling what looked like a footlocker out toward the street. She watched while he hoisted it into his truck and then drove away. A few minutes later, Emily and her brother came out, each carrying briefcases. She watched them get into Emily's car and drive away in the same direction as Alex had.

The lights in Stu's cabin were still on, leading her to think that they were planning to return, and why wouldn't they? Why was it even a question? They were, after all, in the process of moving, so there would likely be many more trips in and out with boxes for the next several weeks. Besides, Alex had already told her he would be there tonight.

When she got in her skiff, she checked it over thoroughly, finding nothing unusual except for a crumpled business card from the local car wash, upon which had been scribbled a phone number with an area code outside Alaska. She tucked it into her pocket with plans to give it to the police when she got home.

Frustrated by the whole situation and realizing just how close she had come to harm, she opened the throttle and took off across the bay with so much speed that the nose of the raft pointed almost straight up, causing Thor to have to huddle beside her to keep from falling overboard.

Chapter Thirty-Nine
Enough Already

To say that she was fed up was an understatement. Mara Benson had been through enough *stuff* in the past several years to have completely passed the saturation point for angst absorbable in any one lifetime.

This time, though, instead of feeling overwhelmed and defeated—this time she was just plain mad. Lessis was at the bottom of this and his actions today had proven it. She hadn't liked him since day one. No wonder every subsequent encounter had left her feeling creepy and tainted by the aura of his sleazy existence.

No matter how politely he had talked or how expensive the suits were that he had worn, no matter how many credentials he had displayed, or how many titles and connections he had flaunted, she had always known deep down inside there was something sinister and disturbing about him. From day one she had tried to keep him at arm's length, and today was proof that the little voice inside her had been right. Never, though, had she imagined that he would actually go so far as to come to her house.

Maybe that is why she had felt the need to carry a gun—not that it had served her well when she needed it. And, poor Thor—he was shaken, she could tell. He knew evil when he saw it. Thank God he had listened to her. He had already been shot once in his life, and to have it happen again would have been more than she could take.

Why Stu had seemed so clocked in to Lessis's comings and goings was its own mystery. The two seemingly had nothing in common, yet Stu had been the first to tell her how Lessis operated as a policeman, and he had known all the details about Lessis leaving the force for a job at the bank long before it became common knowledge in the community.

Lessis, himself, had fawned over Stu's deceased self at the memorial, scattering his pitiful tribute to him within his lengthy and embarrassing self-adulation speech.

Lessis was creepy from any angle you looked at him. Now she understood just exactly what it had been about him that had precipitated such a strong negative emotion in her. Even though the man had made many friendly overtures—and who could fault someone for trying to at least doctor up their appearance with clothing and cologne even though in this case, there was no accounting for taste—she had been repelled by him.

She really didn't want to be thinking about him right now anyway. She had come out here to relax. Lessis was in jail, and whatever it was that had prompted him to run would come out soon. About one thing she was sure, though, hers and Alex's missing money and the charges against Joe Michael were all tied up in Lessis's duplicity.

When she got home and tied her boat up that night, she took Thor for a walk before turning in, taking extra pains to secure her locks and make sure her pistol was within arm's reach. A message from Doug saying that the weather system in Cordova was expected to prevail for at least the next several days felt strangely like a relief. She was okay, and for now she just wanted to sleep, so she called him back and told him just that, thankful when her words seemed to reassure him.

Despite feeling tired from her day out on the water, sleep eluded her. Thoughts—racing, galloping thoughts that seemed to merge into something that almost made sense and then dissipate, racked her brain. It was as though she could just about put it all together, whatever *it* was, before the final answer, the final piece to the puzzle of this latest assault on her life, faded from her mind's eye.

When sleep did come, it was fitful and then deep. When she awoke, like a kindled flame, the jumbled embers of recent events ignited into a burning quest for the truth. Taking her cup of Kona out onto the deck, she sat in the morning fog and rolled the feather between her thumb and fingers as she remembered the words Joe Michael had spoken when handing it to her: *The worst is closer than you think.*

As your own strength grows,
mine will begin to fade.
As before, keep this to protect your future
but this time it will be from my past.

Thor's restless pacing broke her concentration. Placing her empty crystal mug in the sink, Mara Benson pulled on her knit cap, down jacket, and rubber boots before snapping on Thor's leash to take him outside.

Halfway along the trail that led up the hill a few blocks from her cabin, she knew what she had to do. Although it would only be a start, she would be talking to the acting manager at the bank and launching a formal inquiry into all records pertaining to Alex, herself, and the *Driftfeather*—but first she would need to get Alex's consent. She would let the law work out any criminal issues with Lessis, but she wanted to be first in line to get her questions answered, both for her sake and for Alex's.

Chapter Forty
Heart-wrenching Discovery

As Mara approached her cabin, something told her to check to make sure she had tied the skiff up securely yesterday when she had been so tired. Instead of climbing down through the trap door from her deck, she walked past Stu's old place to the end of the dock and then down the floating ramp to look underneath the pilings, where she saw Alex pulling away from his cabin in his own skiff.

She liked that he and Emily lived next door and felt happy that she had helped him find a lifestyle that would suit them both. She gave him a friendly wave, but he had his back to her as he sped away. Maybe she would check on Emily and the two could spend some time together. It might even be a good time to find out how Emily was doing with the pregnancy and let her know she planned to throw a baby shower when it was closer to her delivery time.

Thor ran up ahead, and as if reading her mind, stopped in front of Alex and Emily's cabin, pushing slightly on the door and causing it to open just a crack.

"Thor! Come back here!" Mara hissed, trying not to make a scene, while snapping a leash on him when he did, and pulling him along the boardwalk toward home.

As she and Thor passed the cracked door, she reached to pull it shut, trying hard to do it silently so as not to disturb or frighten Emily. Instead, it was she who was surprised upon hearing a man's voice inside.

"It's probably her brother," she said to no one, pausing to be sure she had heard what she thought she had.

Then she heard Emily.

"I love you so very much, Paul. We'll be through this soon. I just need to give Alex a little more time to . . ."

Was something going on with Alex? He had been acting weird lately. Not his usual fun-loving self.

She stepped back, not wanting to eavesdrop, but when the man spoke again—his voice deep with emotion—she was unable to not hear his words.

"After this we'll always be together, Emily. There'll be no more times like this. Before long it will be just the two of us and soon, our baby."

Mara scurried to her own cabin and slid inside the door feeling as if her heart would burst. Alex had told her that Emily's brother's name was Kent, not Paul. Who was in there with Emily and what did he mean by "our baby?"—as if the statement itself really left any doubt.

Her thoughts were racing toward the irrational. She had worked so hard to stop that kind of thinking, but now the anxiety she had so long fought to overcome had come roaring back. Was this how it had been with Doug and Erin? She tried to stop her crazy thoughts, but found herself wanting to run to Alex to tell him the truth and spare him from going through what she had with Doug.

Calm yourself, Mara. Alex is not Doug and Emily is not you, and this situation is not the same as the one you and Doug went through. She took a deep breath. Why was she reacting this way? Besides, she and Doug were back on track, so why even think of what had gone on before and had been resolved between them?

Just then the phone rang and it was Doug. Everything was fine with him, so she spilled out the details of what had just happened, telling him she wasn't sure what to do.

"Don't go jumping to conclusions, Mara. Besides, it's none of your business."

"But Alex is my friend."

Still, after they talked it all over, Doug had to admit that if he were in Alex's shoes, he would probably—as hard as it would be to hear—want to know.

"Or maybe you should ask Emily about it first."

"I'll try to pick a time that feels right," she told Doug before hanging up.

Meanwhile, when she got up to close the door, Emily and Kent were standing on the dock just to the left of her door, just breaking away from what looked like a very warm embrace. So where then was Paul, and why was Emily hugging her brother? Something had to be wrong.

"Mara," Emily said.

"Hi, Emily—Kent, sorry to interrupt."

"Kent was just . . ."

"Oh, my water's boiling over on the stove," Mara lied, quickly shutting the door and leaving the two standing there.

Before long, she heard a truck drive away and heard Emily's own door latch shut. Did Kent know about Paul? Did everyone but Alex know about Paul?

About two hours later, still sitting at her table trying to decide what to do, she heard the sound of Alex's skiff pulling in under his cabin and felt her own heart flip-flop a couple of times. Did Alex even have a clue? Maybe that was why he had been acting so strangely lately. Maybe he knew already and she wouldn't have to be the one to tell him about Emily and Paul—whoever Paul was—and about the fact that Emily's baby was not his.

On the other hand, what if he didn't know? Maybe she should wait for Doug to get home before facing Alex with the news—just in case his reaction was as unpredictable as his behavior had been as of late. But that could be days away, so she took a deep breath and tried to plan just how she would say the words she needed to say.

Chapter Forty-One
Who's Who?

Alex's reaction to the news about Emily was a surprise.

"I know about Emily and Paul, Mara."

Well, she certainly hadn't expected that! She stared at him, dumbfounded.

"Emily told me you saw her hugging Kent on the dock yesterday, and that earlier you may have heard her talking to someone named Paul. It's not what you think."

Mara stopped herself from responding. Poor Alex.

"There's something you need to know," he said. "Actually, there's several somethings you need to know. Can we meet up this afternoon and I'll explain everything?"

"Okay, Alex. It's really none of my business. All I really wanted to do was to ask your permission to formally request that the bank launch an investigation into what has been going on with your account for the *Driftfeather.*"

"Well, just to give you a quick answer, it goes without saying that of course I will give it to you. I mean, we're business partners, aren't we? And you took a huge risk on me, using your own money. But I'd like to ask you to at least wait until we can talk about this in more detail later today."

"Okay. I had hoped you would agree to my idea. The thing with Emily and you—well, like I said, it's really none of my business and I apologize if I spoke out of line."

"No apology needed, Mara. I'll see you this afternoon—right here—say, about three?"

"See you at three."

~~~

That was weird. Alex hadn't seemed at all disturbed by the news about his wife. Maybe Doug was right, maybe she had jumped to conclusions. When three o'clock rolled around, she was waiting for him on her deck, surprised when he showed up with both Emily and Kent.

"Would any of you like some coffee—or soda, or water?" she said, getting up.

"No, thanks, Mara. Sit down, okay?" Alex said.

Boy, wasn't he all business today.

"Look closely at this," he said, passing his driver's license across the table.

She glanced at the name. It was his, but there was a small mark in the shape of a shield beside it, one she had never seen on her own licenses or anyone else's.

"Well, all I notice is this mark. Does it mean something special?"

"Keep reading," Alex insisted.

The address matched the one she had for him. The picture was the usual stark rendition placed on driver's licenses that most everyone she knew hated. There was one restriction saying that he needed glasses to drive, but aside from that, it looked like a normal driver's license.

"I don't see anything but that mark," she said. "What does this have to do with anything?"

"Look at the birth date, Mara."

"It says your birthday is May 31," she answered. "Is that it? Are you trying to tell me I forgot your birthday, because I am so sorry and I'll make it up to you."

She glanced at the date marker on her watch. Gosh, was it already June 3?

She looked at Emily, who was sitting stone-faced next to Kent, and whose expression she couldn't read because his eyes were hidden behind a pair of aviator sunglasses. Neither of them moved except that Emily shifted slightly in her chair.

"Look at the year, Mara, then do the math," Alex continued.

"What's going on here, Alex?" she demanded, growing tired of whatever game it was the three of them were playing with her.

"First of all, as you can see, I'm not twenty-four," he began. "As a matter of fact, I'm thirty-four, but I've always looked young for my age."

Mara was stunned. Why had Alex lied to her about his age?
~~~

Suddenly he flashed the boyish grin she was so used to. Was he trying to make light of the situation or what, because she was definitely not laughing at this latest surprise?

"Where're you going with this, Alex? I don't know if I even want to hear this," she said, jumping up. "Is this some kind of practical joke or what?"

"It's no joke, Mara," he said, suddenly regaining the serious demeanor he had arrived with.

"If this is about us being closer in age and . . . you're making me . . . where're you going with this? What about you, here, Emily? Is this some kind of weird . . . I don't know . . . and both of you know I'm back with Doug . . ."

"It's nothing at all like that, Mara. Just listen up," Alex assured her, while Emily's expression remained unchanged.

She fought a sudden urge to flee.

"Frankly, Alex, as much as I appreciate your attempt to be honest, or transparent, or whatever it is you're trying to do here . . ."

"It's something like that—," he started to respond.

"If this is about the money, then I'll just write it off. If you're trying to tell me something weird about your past, let's just keep that your little secret."

"Mara," he interrupted her, "I'm with the FBI."

His words stopped her dead in her tracks. Not again. Not this. She spun around, facing him.

"The FBI. Right, Alex. Well, I'll give it to you, I've attracted the Palmer police, the Alaska State Troopers, the International Police Association, so why not the FBI? What sinister plot is unveiling now?" she said, rolling her eyes, then feeling foolish about her childlike response. "You know my history. Why are you doing this to me?"

"Stop it, Mara," he said, reaching into his back pocket to pull out his wallet. Stepping forward, he showed her his badge.

"You can buy those on the Internet," she snapped.

He sat back down, while she paced the room.

"The situation with Joe Michael," he continued. "I've known about it for several months starting—well, actually starting—about two months before I met you."

She looked back at him and said nothing. How could any of this be happening again? She stared at him for what seemed like minutes before asking, "And Emily?"

"FBI," he answered. "The wedding was fake, but the pregnancy—that's real."

"My real name is Anna Pauline Sinclair," Emily said, speaking for the first time since her arrival, "but please call me Annie."

"And this guy here, the man staying with us, who you saw embracing Emily on the dock yesterday, is really her husband and fellow agent, Paul Sinclair," Alex said. "I only told you he was Emily's brother, Kent, so his moving in with us would not arouse suspicion."

Mara watched Paul Sinclair remove his glasses and nod slightly, his mouth curving into a brief half smile, before putting the glasses back on.

"Sorry to alarm you this morning," Paul said in a voice that was more businesslike than apologetic.

"So that explains seeing them leave with briefcases right after you left with the footlocker the other night," Mara said, looking at Alex.

"I didn't know you saw that," he said.

Apparently, everything about Alex had been a lie.

"And your lovely parents? Not really Hollywood stars?" she asked him.

"That part was true, Mara. They are Hollywood stars. How do you think I got to be such a good actor?" he laughed. "But Winron is my mother's maiden name. My real name is Jacob Alexander Phillips, but I've been called Alex my entire life. That little emblem next to my name is to alert law enforcement that I am undercover. And my father is in great health. There was no stroke. I know you were worried."

"I'm relieved to know they're okay," was all she could think of to say before grabbing Thor's leash from the hook on the wall and heading for the door.

"C'mon, Thor. Let's go for a walk."

Chapter Forty-Two
Facing It Alone

When she returned an hour later, the three agents were standing on the dock outside her cabin.

"We decided to go for a sandwich," Annie Sinclair said. "We could see you needed some space."

"How kind of you," Mara said sarcastically, opening her door and unhooking Thor's leash so he could go inside.

"We'd like to finish," Alex said.

"By all means, please come in," she answered.

She took her sweet time before joining them on the deck, stopping first to get Thor some water, then making herself her own sandwich, which she carried outside.

"Since you already ate, I hope you don't mind if I do?"

Annie Sinclair smiled sympathetically, but Alex and Paul were all business as Alex began to speak.

"That footlocker that you saw me with, Mara, holds the final proof of Joe Michael's innocence," he began.

How she wished Doug were here. She needed him now more than ever, but he wouldn't be back for at least a week, so this time she was going to have to face whatever this was alone.

"Here's how it all unfolded," Alex continued. "It's long and it's complicated, but the bottom line is that Joe Michael is innocent, you're innocent and, although I'm not who you thought I was, I'm innocent of doing anything to hurt you. I'm just sorry, knowing your past, that it was you who had to get caught up in this."

Why not me? she wondered, her mind drifting to part of the words Joe Michael had written in the envelope with the second feather.

. . . keep this
to protect your future,
but this time
it will be
from my past.

She listened as Alex began to recount the details of just what had gone on, starting with when she had first moved to Juneau.

"Stu had been bragging around town about how he was finally going to be able to help the daughter from whom he had been estranged most of her life."

"Della," Mara said.

"Stu had also begun bad-mouthing his brother, Joe, around town quite a bit, saying that he'd show him up for thinking he was a 'no account.' That's what Stu said his brother called him, a 'no account.'

"Until then, no one that we talked to had even known that Stu had a brother. Everyone thought he was just a crotchety old loner who probably had some kind of past, just like most everyone in Alaska seems to have as far as I can see. Strange bunch up here sometimes . . ."

Alex chuckled, before resuming his serious demeanor.

"What does that have to do with you, the FBI, and most of all, with me?" Mara asked, ignoring the fact that Alex had just revealed himself to not be of the kindred spirit that binds those who choose to live in the far north that she loved so much—an unshared thought that somehow he intuitively picked up on.

"I'm sorry, Mara. I didn't mean to come across as some kind of a snob. I've loved my time here in Alaska . . ."

She looked away, unsmiling.

"It's beautiful here," Annie murmured, while her husband shifted uncomfortably in his chair.

"Let's get back to business here," Alex said. "Originally, we had been called in by a bank examiner because of his suspicions about a large volume of deposits being put into an account held in the name of Joe Michael—deposits that were not reflected in actual growth to Joe Michael's account on the balance sheet."

"Okay, so Joe Michael can't have a bank account?" Mara said, feeling defensive after hearing Alex's slight against Alaskans. "Maybe he was taking the money out as fast as he was putting it in. Maybe he had automatic payments being taken out—like for medications, or his truck, or something. Why was someone monitoring Joe Michael's account in the first place?"

"The fact of the matter was that large amounts of money were going into the account, and regular withdrawals were being made using savings withdrawal slips signed with the name Joe Michael. The fact that the same exact amount of money was turning up in a second account held in a fictitious name that had the same account number as Joe's, but was held by at least one other branch of Smith Bank, was what prompted the attention of an independent auditor during a routine audit.

"That's when the examiner was called in and what he found in reviewing Joe's account, along with similar irregularities in several other accounts at three separate Smith Bank branches. As a matter of fact, the holders of some of those accounts were already reporting those very irregularities.

"Money from that fictitious account was also being regularly withdrawn using savings withdrawal slips signed with the fictitious name linked to that account. Coincidentally, deposits into an account held by Stu Michael increased substantially from his previous deposit pattern right around that time—but not in the large amounts that ended up being unaccounted for, which further clouded the picture."

"This is all so much to absorb," Mara said. "I feel like my brain is just shutting down trying to understand it all."

"I can see where anyone would find this confusing," Alex said. "It's a very complex crime that took us months to figure out. Maybe we should break for about an hour and meet back here at, say, five and I'll try to make it a little clearer?"

Mara watched as everyone got up and moved through her cabin and out the door. She saw Alex hesitate, as if he wanted to say something, but a glance from Paul had him continue his exit, leaving her standing there wondering what possibly could be next.

Chapter Forty-Three
Less Is More, More or Less

Taking her phone out onto her deck, Mara called the hospital as much to check on Joe as to get her mind off the long, drawn out sequence of events that Alex had dropped like a bombshell into her lap.

"Okay, Sal. Thanks for letting me talk to Joe. Thank goodness he's going to be discharged soon, and I think it's a good idea that they want to put him in assisted living for a week first. It's much better to take it slowly—especially with his history."

She hung up and said a silent prayer of gratitude for the news that Joe Michael was going to fully recover. She hadn't really discussed his arrest much with him, except that Sal had mentioned, and Joe had nodded his head in agreement on the day that Doug had bailed him out of jail, that he knew nothing of any account in his name at Smith Bank.

When Alex returned, she was still sitting on her deck, trying to piece it all together in a way that made some kind of sense. Together, they waited silently for Emily and Kent—well, Annie and Paul, that is—to arrive, neither of them comfortable now that the truth about Alex's identity had been revealed. About fifteen minutes later, Annie and Paul walked out onto her deck.

"Sorry we're late," Annie said.

"As I already said, and getting back to where we were when we took our break," Alex began, "money in six other accounts began to disappear with customers complaining of coming up short—all within the same time frame of about six months.

"At first the discrepancies were just minor, twenty or thirty dollars here or there, but over time, the discrepancies became larger with the dollar amounts corresponding to deposits made into Joe Michael's account, and then later, withdrawn and deposited into the fictitious account.

"When the activity continued well past the initial complaint period, it was then suspected that Joe Michael was involved in some kind of banking scheme, and the FBI was asked to investigate him. It was during that investigation that they found the deposit receipts in Joe Michael's glove box."

"I'm no cop," Mara said, "but I think it's pretty obvious that someone framed Joe, and it looks more and more like that someone was Stu."

She had pretty much had enough of all this blah, blah, blah. Joe was innocent. She was innocent, Alex was a fake, and Stu was a scammer. Even she could figure that out, so why couldn't they just wrap this up?

"As far as we can tell, Stu's involvement was only that he stole his brother's ID and supplied it to an accomplice, who we now believe was Lessis—well, that, and accepting the stolen money that was diverted into his account."

"Oh, yeah, Lessis," she murmured.

"Did you say something, Mara?" Alex asked.

"No. I apologize for interrupting. I do want to point out, though, that when I talked to Joe, after they arrested him, he said he had no idea there was an account in his name at Smith Bank."

"That's because Stu put his own address down as Joe's, so all the statements from the bank would go directly to him. You're right in thinking that Joe never even knew that the account existed and we have been able to independently substantiate that he had no history at all with Smith Bank."

"Like I said," Mara sighed. "Too bad nobody figured this out before they put Joe through the trauma of being arrested."

"Well, no one knew then what we know right now," Alex said. "You can thank Lessis for that. He arranged it all. As you already know, once we obtained a search warrant to investigate Joe's properties, we found the receipts."

"We also found the same statements in Stu's cabin, making it evident that someone was creating duplicates," Paul Sinclair interjected. "That someone was Lessis. It was Lessis who framed Joe, not Stu. Stu's only role was in setting up the account in Joe's name—something he figured Joe would never even find out about. As far as Stu was concerned, all the receipts were coming to him instead of Joe just as planned."

"But Lessis wasn't even there yet?" Mara said, "So why didn't the previous bank manager catch all this?"

"The answer, again, is Lessis," Alex replied. "During the investigation, we learned that Lessis, through his work as a police officer, had something on the bank manager and threatened to expose him if he didn't cooperate with setting up the blind account and then divert that money into Stu's account. It was brilliant, really, since none of the tellers would ever have any reason to become suspicious."

"And how then did Stu get enough money to pay for Della's surgery?" Mara asked.

"I think I'll let Paul explain this," Alex said. "Paul."

"Lessis had already planned to leave the police department, so he further blackmailed the then manager, again threatening to expose him if he didn't hire him as his assistant.

"By the time you moved in, at least according to what Alex gave us as that time frame," Paul said, removing his glasses, "the man you know as Lessis had begun talking about how he would be leaving the police department and managing the local Smith Bank branch for his brother-in-law."

"Yes, that's what I heard," Mara said. "Interesting isn't it, looking back now, that I heard it from Stu?"

"The trouble was . . . is . . ." Paul said, "that Smith Bank is owned by six brothers from Dubai, and that all senior executives are relatives of those six brothers—all Arabs."

Mara could see where this was going as she pictured Lessis's red goatee, but there could be a way . . .

"Maybe his wife was married to one of the Arabs . . ." she said.

"Ever wonder why you never saw Lessis around town with a family?" Alex asked. "Why you never saw the wife whose brother he said ran the bank?"

"I never thought about it, Alex. I guess I was just as happy to see as little of him as possible—starting from that first day when he gave me a ticket for only going five miles over the speed limit on a downhill grade."

Alex and Paul looked at each other and sent a sympathetic look Mara's way.

"First of all, Mara, the man you know as Lessis is divorced from a woman of Scandinavian descent named Inga," Paul continued, "and we have been unable to locate any brother-in-law who worked for Smith Bank or any other bank."

"You've got to be kidding me," Mara said, sitting down. "So how did Lessis get the job at the bank without being thoroughly investigated? I mean, he was a cop, you figure he would have checked out as A-okay and all that."

"Here is what we pieced together after talking to employees of the bank and the former bank manager, who is also now in custody on unrelated charges." Paul continued. "Apparently Lessis was originally hired as assistant manager by the then manager under the same threat Lessis had used to expose him when forcing him to set up the blind account in Joe's name.

"Later, after getting hired, Lessis used his contacts at the police department to turn the manager in, making himself look like a hero and a shoo-in to replace the outgoing manager—a scheme that worked perfectly for him in securing that job."

"So you're saying that he knew the 'right' people and then he slid into the position because he looked like he had been a hero to the bank." Mara said. "Wow!"

"It was the classic double-cross," Paul said. "Further investigation on Lessis—fingerprints, handwriting, and some other things—revealed his real identity to be Lester S. Moore. Les S. Moore—and not the famous architect either—who is wanted in three states for parole violation from a 1986 felony conviction for embezzling funds from an investment firm in California."

"Wow!" Mara gasped. "Lessis stuck it to everyone."

"It's complicated," Alex said. "The fact that Stu and Lessis seemed to be on pretty friendly terms was suspicious, because the two appeared to have nothing in common and were never seen together around town—at least from what we have been able to determine through the many interviews we did with people who knew one or the other of them, or knew them both. The only connection here seems to be that both Stu and Lessis were opportunists, and this time their goals worked well together."

"You know, I don't know about anyone else, but I'm just exhausted," Annie said.

"I think we all are," Paul added. "How about if we all get some sleep and meet up for coffee in the morning. You can finish filling us in then, Alex."

"Sounds good," Alex replied.

By the time Mara went to bed, she had already had two glasses of wine and read all of the news on three different online websites. Nothing she saw there even compared to the story that was unfolding right here in her own small world.

Chapter Forty-Four
What Really Happened Here?

As she sat in the drizzle of a Juneau morning the next day, Mara thought about everything she had been told the day before. By now it was easy to see that this was about a lot more than just Stu and his violation of his brother's good name. Again, her thoughts shifted to Joe's prophetic words. He had tried to warn her in the best way he could that somehow, on some level, their lives were linked together in a bond that affected them both. The story she was hearing could easily be viewed as unbelievable, but she knew that it wasn't.

When Alex called suggesting she meet them all at his place around noon, she almost felt relieved—like maybe hearing this away from her own home would make it all less traumatic. When she got to Alex's place, she joined him, Annie, and Paul in the living room, since the drizzle outside had now turned to a heavy downpour.

As each of them talked in turn, she listened, giving her full attention to Alex, Paul, and the woman she now knew as Annie.

"So, none of this was really about me," she stated.

"No, you were just pulled into it through your association with me," Alex said, "and the details of that association are a whole other story—some of which you understand even more than my colleagues do, Mara."

She smiled at the obvious reference to both their friendship and business partnership. Maybe she hadn't misjudged Alex as much as she thought she had.

"The fact that you just happened to know Joe Michael and his brother, Stu, as well as Della, is something that I will always find to be among the most incredible coincidences in my work in law enforcement," he continued, appearing a bit more emotional than previously. "It's almost as if there is some plan of destiny and some connecting life force running as a common thread through the whole situation—but we don't normally think that way at the FBI, so let's just leave it that this is my own personal, unscientific feeling and move on. Can you take this, Paul?"

"Specifically, what we think happened is that Stu then stepped things up by assisting Lessis in getting information on Alex Winron's account for the *Driftfeather* so that money could be siphoned out of that account—information Stu obtained about Alex by breaking into your cabin—well, not breaking in, but using the key in your lockbox to get in after somehow stealing your code."

So that explained why her lockbox had been left unlocked that one day she had gone out in her raft, and also why Stu was standing by her front door looking sheepish when she got home that same night. Perhaps it also explained his actions in taking the logbook on the *Driftfeather* the first time they had all sailed out together, thus validating that he had no clue that Alex Winron was any other than a young fisherman buying his first seiner.

Mara's head was spinning. How in the world did she get into these situations? Was this some kind of a joke, or something? Hadn't she been through enough weird scenarios since arriving in Alaska for any ten lifetimes?

"So, how does this involve me?" she asked Alex, again. "You know, other than the fact that my cabin was apparently entered to steal information about you?"

"Well, it goes without saying that it involves you because it involves me as your business partner," Alex spoke up. "The rest of it—the links with Joe, Stu, and Della—coincidence, unless you choose to subscribe to the destiny theory I alluded to earlier . . ."

"It seemed like the perfect setup," Paul continued. "The previous bank manager, under threat from Lessis, had set things up so there would be no way to trace the discrepancies or the missing money directly to either Stu or Lessis except that Stu was 'helping out' his brother by depositing money for him.

"Transaction reports would look legitimate with all the money except for the payoff to Stu going into the blind account, and the amount diverted to Stu metered out in small, regular deposits so as to make them look legitimate—like a pension payment or something like that. As a matter of fact, our investigation shows that checks that resembled a fabricated pension fund were regularly deposited into Stu's personal account. The one thing that Stu didn't know was that Lessis was diverting the greatest share of the money to himself, giving Stu only enough to make him think he was getting over."

"And so Stu just let the money keep rolling in," Mara said, shaking her head in disgust.

"For Stu, it was all about Della," Alex said simply. "Stu was simply desperate to make things right with the daughter he abandoned at birth."

"And for some reason, he waited until he was an old retired man to do it, not to mention that in the whole time I knew him, he never once mentioned a daughter, or any other family for that matter," she said.

"Stu knew he was dying," Annie said. "What started out as a simple scam had gotten him in too deep. He had already accepted over a hundred thousand dollars of illegal money into his account. By the time he figured that out, he had become a hero to his long lost daughter and had nothing to lose and everything to gain by letting her believe he was the good person he wanted her to think he was."

"It was all set up so that no one would know that Stu was part of the scheme," Paul said. "Stu could look good to his daughter—help her with her surgery by using his brother, who in Stu's mind would never find out."

"Apparently they didn't figure on Joe being arrested," Mara said.

"Joe's arrest, although more than any of them bargained for, gave Lessis, Stu, and the other manager the security of believing that they were above suspicion—that is until Lessis turned on the old manager, who then turned state's evidence in a plea bargain and blew the whole case wide open, including the fact that Lessis was pocketing most of the money," Paul continued.

"So, in the end, Lessis stuck it to Stu, too," Mara said.

"Basically, he did," Alex answered, "although by then Stu was out of state with Della and died a short time later. No one is sure if Stu ever realized the extent of the crime."

"Couldn't Stu see Lessis for what he was? Didn't he consider that he might get caught?" she asked.

"Stu was blinded by his need to outshine Joe," Alex said. "He was known by everyone in his circle for making comments that Joe 'had it all' inferring that his brother never had to face the hardships and struggles with which Stu viewed his own life. Joe was never affected financially. Only his identity was used to open the fake account. The money was taken from me, you, and the six others whose accounts were compromised."

"Quite simply, Stu never thought he would get caught and he never thought that Joe would either," Paul said.

"Stu and Joe had been estranged ever since the fire that took both their wives' lives," Annie said. "The fact that Joe Michael stepped up to the plate and cared for Stu's daughter after the fire irked Stu. As you know, Della's mother was Stu's wife and Joe Michael's wife's twin sister, so Joe, being the good man that he is, took on the responsibility that Stu never would after the fire. In Stu's eyes, that made him look bad."

"What a troubled man Stu must have been inside," Mara said.

"It's just the way he thought. Stu knew he had cancer. We figure that because Lessis was so slick and so cunning in the way that he used people, Stu had no idea he had gotten in so deep and was banking on being dead before he was discovered if he ever was. Fortunately for him, he was—dead before being discovered, that is."

"Just how deep are we talking, Alex?"

"Deep enough that some of the money siphoned off the fake account set up by Lessis, using information about Joe's identity provided by Stu, was being used to support a growing terrorist organization within our own country—something we discovered by accident while investigating the phone number that Lessis dropped in your skiff."

Suddenly Mara felt cold—tired and cold. She took several deep breaths and pulled her sweater up tight under her chin.

"Joe tried to warn me," she said limply. "Not in the way you think, Alex—or whatever your name is."

"You mean about the terrorist organization?" Paul said.

"No, just that something bad was coming down."

She went on to explain the feather and the note to him and the others, along with the history of the first feather and all that had gone on before, stopping when everyone but Alex seemed lost and uninterested in such unscientific hypotheses.

"The place you came in, Mara—the way this affects you," Alex continued, "is that you just happened to move in next door to Stu right when the FBI was called in. We were getting close to closing in on Lessis when you told me you were ready to launch your own investigation. We had to step in and stop you. You had no idea we were about to move in on Lessis and we just couldn't let you shake things up right at this critical moment in our case."

"And the fact that Lessis was a police officer—he must have had a background check for that job," Mara said.

"Stolen ID, pure and simple," Annie said. "That's why he didn't stay on the force very long. Embezzlement had always been his game. He just took the police job to get comfortable in the community and legitimize himself."

"What happens now?" Mara asked.

"What happens now is that you will be called on to testify about your relationship with Alex Winron and your own attempts to clear up the scenario that ultimately will be revealed to be Lessis's and Stu's embezzlement of Alex's and your money," Paul said.

"And what about Joe?"

"Joe's name will be cleared during the course of the trial. I promise you that we have a strong enough case to put Lessis away for a very long time," Alex said. "When all the evidence is presented, there will be no doubt that Joe Michael was simply a victim of identity theft, especially since I found these hidden in a niche in the wall in Stu's cabin."

Mara looked at the pile of disentangled papers that Alex handed her. Each had been placed in individual Baggies marked as evidence. In her hands were dozens of deposit receipts to Joe Michael's account.

"I took these out of Stu's cabin the other night," Alex said. "I found them stuffed behind a loose log in his bedroom."

"So that explains the footlocker . . ."

"I was surprised when you told me earlier that you had seen me."

"I saw you from my raft. At first it seemed strange, but then I convinced myself that you were only moving some of your things early since I knew you and Emily were leaving Alaska."

Mara smiled weakly at Alex, but he was all business. It was at that moment she knew that this was real, and that any connection she had had with Alex Winron the young fisherman, had simply been an elaborate ruse set up by law enforcement. She had been here before—too many times and with too many others.

"Fingerprints will reveal no evidence that Joe Michael ever touched these receipts," Paul said. "Joe is innocent. As a matter of fact, I received information this morning that charges against him are being dropped.

"Joe will need to testify, but the fact that he was not even in Southeast Alaska on the dates of any of these deposits—information supported by witnesses and our investigation—have pretty much exonerated him from any wrongdoing. That and a confession from Lessis."

"Lessis confessed?"

"It was part of a plea bargain, but thanks to the new information that you supplied, we got him on the larger charge of interstate fraud and terrorism," Alex told her. "Guess he had a soft spot for you after all."

"What do you mean by that?" she asked.

"He told me he knew how much Joe Michael and even Stu meant to you. He said he had heard the story about Della and the shooting at the motel. He also said he was touched by the memorial you got together for Stu after he died."

"Really," she said. "I always felt he didn't like me."

"Lessis really didn't want either Joe or Stu to get hurt. He was just using them. He set everything up so it would be almost impossible to incriminate either of them—not that he was going to resist letting it happen if somehow that came down—but he tried to make it so that they would stay off the radar, if you will.

"As for you, he said he figured you had already been through enough. He called you a decent person. It goes to show that you never know, doesn't it—you know, about how someone thinks? I never would have taken a guy like him for someone with either a heart or a conscience. It's also why he probably didn't kill you when he had the chance."

Mara turned pale. For the first time, Alex's description of Lessis's actions had made her actually think about her violent encounter with the man she knew only as a sleazy bank manager and former cop.

"One more thing, Alex," she said softly. "Why did the FBI let it go this far?"

"Our divisions in other states were investigating their own compromised accounts at Smith Bank. Until about a week ago, they hadn't found any way to link Lessis to those accounts. That is, until Stu died. When Stu's fake account in Joe's name and his own actual account were closed out and then the same account numbers reappeared in at least two other branches of Smith Bank, everyone started looking for a common link, especially when Lessis was promoted to general manager of both of those branches. After all, Lessis was a hero to everyone at the bank for exposing the old manager—a man whose word could not be trusted once it was revealed he had engaged in interstate child pornography, which is what Lessis had on him."

"Wow!" Mara said, "and nobody suspected anything before this? Nobody at Smith Bank?"

"The Arabs wanted to let it play out; they feared some kind of link to some terrorist organization that they assumed would be Al Qaeda, but to everyone's surprise—thanks to you turning in that phone number you found—it turned out to be a homegrown terrorist group hoping to destroy America from within. That ring," Alex said, "has now been exposed and compromised."

Just then Thor wandered out, giving Mara the look that said he wanted to go for a walk.

"Go ahead, Mara," Alex told her. "You need some time to absorb all of this. Just be sure not to talk about this to anyone, not even Doug, for now. I'll get back with you tomorrow to fill you in on what happens next. It's all going to come down pretty fast—the case is that strong."

Chapter Forty-Five
Closure . . . Almost

. . . Mara Benson Edwards Williams Benson . . .

. . . the truth, the whole truth, and nothing but the truth, so help me, God . . .

. . . yes, I recognize the defendant as former Juneau police officer and Smith Bank Manager, K. Lessis . . .

. . . yes, I do live at . . . and, yes, that is the cabin directly north of the one formerly occupied by Mr. Stuart Michael . . .

. . . yes, I do know Della . . . and Joe M . . .

. . . yes, this is the deposit slip I made out on . . .

. . . yes, I recognize this man as Alex Winron . . .

. . . yes, I did propose a business relationship with Mr. Winron involving the F/V *Driftfeather* . . .

~~~

The trial, although stressful, was mercifully short. As Alex had predicted, Lessis was convicted on multiple counts of embezzlement—identity theft, fraud, blackmail, interstate money laundering, and a host of other offenses, including domestic terrorism. Mara watched him the day the sentence was handed down. Even though handcuffed, he strutted around as though the guards were his personal staff.

"Looks like he just doesn't get it," Doug whispered in her ear as she linked her free arm through Joe Michael's, who was standing on the other side of her.

"He'll get that smirk wiped offa his face in the slammer," Sal said from the other side of Joe. "Slimy danged . . ."
~~~

Mara stood quietly as Les S. Moore was led from the courtroom. She watched as he clunked along in his orange prison garb, his feet shackled in chains. Just as he passed in front of her, he made a sudden move to wrest himself from the grip that two officers had on his arms before they quickly subdued him and led him away, but not before he looked her squarely in the eye and flashed her a sinister grin, then pursed his lips as if kissing her from across the room.

She felt Doug tense beside her and placed a gentle hand on his arm. He had been shocked to learn of all that had transpired since Mara moved to Juneau and surprised how well she had handled herself around the slimy likes of Lessis.

Fortunately, neither Joe nor Sal seemed to have seen the look.

"Are we still gonna meet up to discuss the seiners?" Doug asked.

"How about if we meet for dinner over at the hotel?" Alex suggested.

"Works for us," Sal said.

"And I just need to check on Thor," Mara said.

"I'll walk him while you get ready," Doug added.

"I'll find Annie and Paul and make reservations for, let's say, seven—that okay?" Alex said.

"You feelin' all right, sweet baby?" Sal said to Joe.

"Feelin' fine enough, Sal," Joe chuckled.

Mara couldn't help but notice the toll the trial and all that went with it had taken on Joe Michael. Not sure just how she would do it; she silently vowed to find a way to bring a sparkle back to the old man's face.

Chapter Forty-Six
Fine Dining

By the time everyone met up in the hotel dining room, a light drizzle had begun to fall. From her place at the large round table near the back of the dining area, Mara nestled into the warmth of the nearby stone fireplace as she watched Joe and Sal come in. Although Sal had often boasted of being "barely 5 feet tall," today she seemed shorter than usual, and frailer, too. Strange how her boisterous ways had always made her seem much taller.

Joe Michael was not much taller than his wife. Mara watched the two shuffle across the room, Sal's arm linked solidly through his. The couple were both on the far side of seventy now, not really old by Alaska standards, but old enough so that they had begun to assume the slightly bent-over stance of the elderly. Joe might even be closer to his mid to late seventies. Hadn't he once told her about how he had joined the army when he was twenty-two and hadn't been sent to Nam until he was twenty-five?

Joe's full head of brown hair was supported by a good growth of gray roots, making Mara smile at his obvious attempt to retain some of the trappings of youth.

"Sal likes me to look good," he had once told her.

Sal's hair was brilliant red and sported an outgrowth of gray roots similar to her husband's. Both wore the shiny blue bomber jackets often worn by members of one of Alaska's oldest fraternal order of pioneers.

Mara smiled, her heart filled with love for the two seniors.

"Hell's a blazin', Jane, whadja do, rush right on over here from the courthouse?" Sal bellowed from halfway across the room.

Mara stood and pulled out two chairs, greeting the couple warmly as they reached her. Just then Doug strode in and joined them, followed only seconds later by Annie, Paul, and Alex.

The conversation was lively, as if they were ignoring the fact that Emily, Kent, and Alex were really FBI agent Alex and his fellow agents Annie and her husband, Paul. Despite the circumstances, there was genuine affection among them, and they enjoyed a hearty meal and a jovial evening together before Annie and Paul left to catch a flight to Seattle. It was then that Alex gathered them all in comfortable chairs around the fireplace to discuss the reason they were really there.

"Now that Les S. Moore has been brought to justice, we can all feel assured that we are safe from further harm," he began, speaking authoritatively in a way that made him seem the stranger to them all that he really was.

"Of course, each of you will receive our agency's assistance in securing your identities and retrieving your assets . . ."

Mara closed her eyes as Alex talked about all the details of the investigation, and about the ways and means that their property and lives would be restored.

While the others sat in rapt attention, her mind wandered to the day that he had shown up outside her cabin and offered to help carry in her table and a few other things.

She had taken him, as she had so often done with most everyone she knew, at face value, little suspecting that he was anyone besides the person he appeared to be.

Once again, she had naively fallen prey to deception. Well, maybe deception was too strong a word. The point was, how could she ever trust her instincts when each time she had, she had been wrong about so many people in her life? She reached into her purse for a breath mint and felt the feather given to her by Joe Michael.

. . . As your strength grows,
mine will begin to fade.
As before, keep this to protect your future,
but this time it will be from my past.

How was it that Joe had known her life would become entwined with Stu's? Wasn't Alex just a bit player in the ongoing saga that had become her life? If so, it wouldn't be fair to blame him for violating her trust. After all, wasn't he just playing his part in her destiny?

"Tell me, Alex," she interrupted him. "Tell me why you went so far as to buy the *Driftfeather*?"

Alex seemed taken aback at the directness of Mara's question. Looking at her, he took a sip of his drink before leaning back in his chair and then leaning forward again to speak.

"It's complicated," he began, "and I can't say too much without revealing some ongoing investigations, but let me try."

Suddenly everyone else stopped talking, all eyes fixed on Alex. Slowly he began to weave together the story of how he had come to purchase the *Driftfeather*, spurred on in part, he told them, by Mara's own bold and timely offer to become his silent partner.

"The government was looking for a way to close in on some of the drug activity going on out in the Aleutians," he told them. "As you know, every summer an influx of people from all over the world come into Alaska to work in the fisheries.

"It's no secret that a fair amount of drug smuggling occurs then, particularly in locations far out and away from population centers. Every summer you read in the paper or hear on TV about another incident where drugs are involved on some fishing vessel or another. What the public hears, well, that's just the tip of the iceberg."

Mara sat silently as Doug and Sal nodded in agreement. She had heard stories from Doug and others about such activities, but had never really paid them much attention.

"The government had been talking about buying a fishing boat to launch a sting operation out at sea," Alex continued. "They wanted something in addition to the well-documented work done by the coast guard, and they wanted something that would allow an investigation to go totally undetected even by the usual government agencies."

"And you were the one?" Doug asked.

"Fishing seiners have always held a great deal of fascination for me," Alex said, "and it's true what I told Mara about wanting to succeed without any financial help from my parents."

Mara nodded. At least one thing Alex had told her had been true.

"When the funding came through right at the time that the *Driftfeather* and Mara's offer to be a silent partner coincided, and right when we were closing in on Lessis and his activities, it all seemed like a destiny-driven sequence of events—almost too perfect, actually—but certainly lining everything up to help us achieve two major objectives at once, that of exposing Lessis, and launching the sting operation at sea."

Mara looked at Joe Michael, who sat unflinching as Alex's story unfolded. Even Sal, who usually had plenty to say, remained silent.

It was Doug who spoke first and expressed the thought that was on everyone else's mind, "And what happens to the *Driftfeather* now?"

"Well, everyone here knows that Mara already owns half the seiner, which means that the government only owns half. The only reason I'm able to talk about this with you now," Alex continued, "is that the government has decided to abandon its efforts with—and therefore its interest in—the *Driftfeather* in exchange for another type of investigation—one that, as you must certainly understand, I am not at liberty to discuss. In the coming weeks they will be actively looking for a way to dump their interest in the seiner."

Mara felt her heart sink as Sal clutched her hand tightly.

"I'll buy the government out, then," Doug spoke up. "Whatever it takes, I'll borrow more money and I'll buy you out. Anything to hold on to the *Driftfeather*."

Alex smiled. "What none of you know is that there is a $250,000 reward for the capture and prosecution of Les S. Moore and his ring of embezzlers. Because of Mara's testimony about the activities of both Lessis and Stu, and Lessis's subsequent conviction, and because of her willingness to risk her own safety in confronting Lessis before we stepped in and stopped her, a determination has already been made that the reward money will go to her."

Mara turned pale, speechless.

"I know this comes as a huge surprise to you, Mara," Alex said, getting up and walking over to give her a hug. "But if anyone deserves this reward, you do. The other thing is that the government has agreed to give you, as half owner of the *Driftfeather*, first option on buying her in full—that is, if that is an option you would like to pursue."

"It is," she said so faintly that she wasn't even sure herself if she had spoken.

"That's exactly what I wanted to hear, because to be honest, Mara, you've proven to be one of the best friends anyone could ever ask for, and if you'll let me, I'd love to go out on the *Driftfeather* with you from time to time, just to get away from my work—of course, if Doug's okay with that," he said laughing.

"More'n okay, friend. Any time. Any place," Doug said.

Suddenly, everyone was laughing as the gathering of the good friends continued well on into the night. Since Alex intended to leave early the next morning, they all said their goodbyes for now.

As for Annie, well, she had played her part as Emily to perfection and she, too, they each agreed, would always be welcome in Juneau or anywhere any of them happened to be—something each of them had emphasized to her before she left, and only after making her promise to let them know as soon as the baby was born—the baby who Annie and Paul agreed would be called Juneau, no matter what its sex was.

Chapter Forty-Seven
To Beach or Not to Beach . . .

Doug helped the pilot load Joe and Sal's gear into the plane at the airport in Juneau, while Mara helped each of them climb up on the struts where they situated themselves inside.

"Doug says we'll be coming in tomorrow," she told them. "I need to go over a few things with my house sitter about KonaJane's, and make sure my raft is tied up securely since we're going to be gone for at least a couple of weeks."

"I appreciate ya lettin' me bring the *Driftfeather* in with ya, Jane," Sal hollered out the door, "and I think Joe's gonna be fine with helpin' Doug with the *Storm Roamer*."

Just in case extra help was needed, Doug had hired Derrk Stanley to help with the *Roamer*, and hired Derrk's son, Josh, to help with the *Driftfeather*. He would captain the *Storm Roamer*, though, and Mara would captain the *Driftfeather*—each of them making sure that both Joe and Sal had all the time they needed at the wheel.

"Ain't captained no seiner for the last twenty years, Jane," Sal laughed nervously, "but guess it's like they say 'bout ridin' a bike, huh?"

"I've got no doubts, Sal. Matter of fact, I'm hoping that watching you will teach me a few things since it seems that Doug and I are now the owners of two seiners."

"Bert, that's my dead first husband, Bert used to do things with that seiner that no one could believe. Many's the time he beached her on some remote island for a few days' R & R," Sal laughed.

Mara smiled. Maybe she and Doug could do something like that. She was sure he had the expertise. In the past he had always concentrated on working and lobbying for fishing issues. Maybe it was time to slow down and actually start enjoying the sea.

As if reading her mind, Doug gave her arm a gentle squeeze as he walked by. It was all going to be okay between them. She was sure of it and felt her heart in her throat at the thought.

Things were a little crazy the first day out, with Sal wound up like a clock at the thought of being at the wheel with only Mara as backup.

"Hell's bells, Jane, maybe I ain't fit fer the job no more, the way I run us off course this mornin'."

Mara had been a bit concerned when they lost sight of Doug and Joe for a few hours, but Josh had worked to get them back on track, teaching both women the finer points of navigating the area.

By the next day, Sal was her old confident self, and by day three there was no dealing with the size of the ego that had emerged once she got her sea legs back.

Mara hadn't laughed so much in a long time, especially when Sal decided to move ahead of Doug and Joe and let the tide carry the *Driftfeather* onto the beach in a small cove along the shore, forcing both Doug and Derrk to do the same once they caught up with them.

"You're one hot little tamale, Sal," Joe chuckled as everyone met along the beach, each in skiffs from the respective seiners.

"What were you thinking, Mara?" Doug admonished her.

"Lighten up," she laughed. "Sal said she's done this before—said she and Bert used to beach here all the time."

"Well, now, I guess we all have. I hope you two women have a plan for getting us back out in deep water."

"Soon as we have lunch, young man," Sal told him. "Ya think yer dealin' with a coupla flea brains here?"

"Won't do no good to argue," Joe told Doug, who nodded his head in agreement before walking the beach to inspect both seiners.

"I guess they're all right. Doesn't mean it couldn't have turned out differently, though."

Mara stifled more laughs for now. Clearly, Doug was concerned for their safety and she loved him for that.

Even Sal sensed the stress she had placed on him. "Guess I got caught up in the fun of it all, Doug. I think it's time to put you back in charge."

Doug hugged the old woman and told her not to worry, meanwhile making arrangements with Derrk to get the *Driftfeather* refloated with the next tide, while he took care of the *Storm Roamer.*

They drifted out without incident during the next high tide and were back in Juneau a week later as planned.

"I ain't had fun like that in years," Sal laughed. "'Bout time my Joe got a taste a the life I used ta lead."

Joe Michael tenderly pinched his wife's cheek and followed it up with a kiss smack on the lips, which set the old woman to laughing more. Now that everyone was safe, Doug, too, joined in the laughter, admitting that he'd always wanted to try something like that but never had the guts.

After taking Derrk and Josh to the airport, he met the others at Mara's cabin.

"How about if we start planning us a wedding?"

Chapter Forty-Eight
Home

Mara woke on the morning of her wedding to the rare treat of seeing the sun stream through the patio window. After getting up to get her coffee, she languished in bed, thinking of how the past year had brought so much unexpected change to her life. When she reached over to get a coaster out of the nightstand drawer, she saw the gun there, right where it had remained since she bought it. Why had she ever thought she needed it? Next to the gun was the feather given to her by Joe Michael. She stroked it and felt the thickness of the paint that formed the two red dots near the top, and twirled it gently as the sun made them glimmer.

Just as the first feather had done, this one had protected her from harm, but had it really been the feather, or had it actually been the fatherly love of Joe Michael that had cast a protective aura around her? She wasn't sure what to do with this feather. Unlike the first one, which she had given to Della, this one seemed to have no more purpose—or did it? Suddenly, she knew. Placing the feather gently back in the drawer, she called for Thor and took him for a long walk, enjoying the special warmth of the morning.

Later, after indulging in a leisurely bath, she and Sal clipped along the sidewalk in their high heels—she hiking her long ivory dress up to clear any puddles, and Sal proudly noticing that her dark purple dress perfectly matched the flowers in Mara's hair.

The small wood-framed cathedral was unimpressive by European or even by Lower 48 standards, but it served a congregation of the faithful with the best the area had to offer. Joe was waiting at the back of the church, where he handed Mara her bouquet after escorting Sal to her seat.

"My own daughter would have been about your age," he told her.

Mara smiled in a way that revealed how touched she was by those words.

"I brought this for you," she said, handing Joe the feather. "I finally figured it out—everything with the feather."

Joe smiled slightly.

"Took you a while, but glad you finally caught on."

"I'm sorry you don't have your own daughter to walk down the aisle right now."

"And you don't have your own father," Joe said. "But between the two of us, we have enough good memories and enough love to have them both here in spirit."

She took Joe's hand and squeezed it before reaching up to dab a tear from his eye with the sleeve of her dress.

"I can't think of a better way to start my new life with the man I love than to have the other man I love walk me to his arms," she said gently.

Taking the feather from Joe's hand, she started to slide it inside the breast pocket of his jacket.

"This is of no use to me unless the love it brought me can be given back to you," she told him. "So, I want you to take it now, because I'm going to be okay."

"I believe you will be," Joe said, but before he could finish pushing the feather all the way into his pocket, the sun caught the red dots and merged them into one, before they completely disappeared leaving the feather in its original state.

For a moment they locked eyes, each caught up in the significance of the moment.

"Let's get you up that aisle so we can both get on with our lives," Joe said with a wink, as he tucked the feather the rest of the way into his pocket and began to escort her along the white runner that led to the altar.

At the far end of the church, Doug watched them, silently thanking Joe for his part in bringing him and Mara back together. Like her, he had no doubt that was exactly how it had come to be.

And Thor carried the ring. Just as he had once found her first wedding ring, he now carried her last one. Mara smiled at seeing the little wiggle he gave when he saw her, and laughed when he nudged his way between her and Doug at the altar.

Later, when Doug and Mara passed Graveyard Island in Hoonah, Joe's totem was lit by a ray of sun that had just broken through the heavy mist. It looked taller than before and untouched by the harsh weather of the area.

Something was different about it and they steered the *Driftfeather* ß shore for a closer look.

No longer was there a feather running up the side of the totem as before. Instead there was an eagle, flying sideways with one wing pointing up and one wing pointing down. And there was no more red dot, only the clear yellow of the eagle's eye, which they could see was made of Russian amber.

For a long time they stood there looking at the totem from the deck of the *Driftfeather*, here back in this place that held such powerful energy—this place from which arose the very essence of unconditional love.

It was here where they had both felt the immense spirit of goodness first brought to them by Joe Michael, and it was here where they now stood as they began their true life together—tested, tempered, and strengthened by not only the worst life could fling their way, but also by their eternal willingness to retain hope in the essential goodness of life.

Mara had found her path. She had emerged as the person she was always meant to be—strong, loving, and pure. She had brought those things with her to Doug, leaving no doubt now about their future as they stood here in the place that had first brought their two hearts together.

On the way back they would stop and visit Sal and Joe, who had decided to build a home right here in Hoonah, and who would be flying in as soon as they locked up Stu's old cabin. Then they would head back to their cabin in Juneau, which they had decided to make home.

And they would do everything in their power to make sure that Joe and Sal would be able to join them midsummer for the party being planned in their honor in Palmer—up Knik River Road at the homestead of Mara's best friend's sister, where so many of their close friends would soon gather to celebrate everything good that had brought them all together in life. They just wouldn't have it any other way.

~~~
~~~

www.ingramcontent.com/pod-product-compliance
Lightning Source LLC
LaVergne TN
LVHW020633100826
845148LV00012B/2166
* 9 7 8 1 5 9 4 3 3 3 1 8 7 *